light

in

Mourning

by

Adriane Leigh

Light in Mourning

Cover Design by Sarah Hansen at Okay Creations

Edited by Hercules Editing and Consulting,

and Karen Lawson

Dedication

To my girls: Your shining eyes and bright smiles bring me so much joy every day.

Tristan

I glanced at the screen of my phone before whipping it across the interior of the Jeep. I heard it land with a thud on the seat. Second time today the crazy bitch had called me and I was so over it. So fucking over it. Apparently, she didn't understand what had happened between us was a one-night-only kinda deal. Don't get me wrong, not that I wasn't flattered that she wanted an encore, a repeat performance—that wasn't even to say I wouldn't have been interested in the past—but it was a different time. This was now, and I wasn't interested.

I'd been back in North Carolina for three weeks. Three weeks of living on my boat. Sleeping on a lumpy bed and showering in a too-tiny boat shower. Three weeks since my closest friend Gavin had dropped me here with a pat on the shoulder and a despondent look on his face. I didn't want his pity; I didn't even want to see his face. There was only one face that played on repeat in my head; one beautiful smile, one pair of deep brown eyes that flashed when she laughed. In the past month, there was only one face I saw when I was buried deep inside someone.

Scratch that.

All fucking summer there was only one face I saw when I was buried inside someone and hers was the only face I could bear to see in the flesh right now. Everyone else looked at me with a flash of pity. Drew tried to talk to me, tried to reassure me, tried to make me understand, but there was no understanding.

Georgia had left.

Georgia had promised it would only be a few days. Fast-forward an entire fucking month without a single call. She was fucking haunting me, and now, here I was, docked on the North Carolina coast because I couldn't fucking get away from her no matter how hard I tried. And truth was, I shouldn't have been surprised. This is exactly what had happened to my dad when my mom left—he'd collapsed into himself. Isolated and pushed all thoughts of happiness away. I understood his coping mechanism now, it's exactly what I was doing.

When I'd returned to Jacksonville a month ago after the hurricane had driven us out of North Carolina, I'd walked into my apartment with a lighter step than when I'd left. I'd had faith that it wasn't over for Georgia and me. We may have had a rough summer—fucking and fighting, stolen glances and heartbreaking moments at the beach house, but we'd grown much too close to let this be the end. I felt her in my bones. She'd been tattooed on my heart.

And then a fucking week went by.

I called her over and over. I sent texts. I'd talked to Georgia's best friend, Drew, to make sure my dark-haired girl was okay. I grew more worried. Finally, after two weeks of nothing, knowing she was alive and well, and just back with Kyle, I threw my hands up. I tossed in the towel, got torn-up drunk, and made a call I never should have made.

Sophie.

Sophie-fucking-Watkins, the very woman I'd been escaping this past spring. She'd tried to call me off and on all summer, sent me random texts and pictures of herself nearly fucking naked and I'd ignored every single one of them. I'd ignored them because there was only one woman I could focus on all summer. Through it all—all the ups and downs, the back and forth, the lies and truth—she consumed my every waking thought.

So when I'd been rip-roaring drunk that night a few weeks ago and made the stupid-ass decision to send Sophie one little text, she'd replied immediately.

I fucked her that night. All night.

I fucked her, trying to fuck another girl out of my system. She was wild, uninhibited, and nearly crazy. Scratch that—completely fucking crazy—but it was hot. It was just too bad my drunken brain had morphed her long blonde hair into chestnut brown, her bright blue eyes into the deepest shade of melted chocolate I'd ever seen. What I was unable to ignore were her high-pitched moans, so I cranked the music on my iPod dock and drowned those out too.

My entire fucking body ached for Georgia and I was looking for an escape. Something to fill the void. To feel like myself again; not someone completely fucking shattered by a woman who hadn't chosen me.

I woke up that morning, tangled up in Sophie, and immediately hated myself. I heaved a desperate sigh and she stirred. Just as her eyes fluttered open, I locked my gaze on her and told her it was time to go. Pain passed across her eyes before they hardened. She called me an asshole and climbed out of bed, throwing her barely-there red dress over her head and stomping out of my apartment.

Fast-forward to fucking now and the crazy bitch hadn't stopped calling.

She called me every single fucking day.

It felt like a rewind of this spring. Sophie riding my ass, and not in the good way. So once again, I found myself in need of an escape. The need to escape Gavin's worried glances, Drew trying to console me about Georgia, and the crazy ass blonde who wanted a repeat. I treated Sophie like shit, I knew that—I'd used her—but what pissed me off more was that she wanted more. She had no self-respect and still wanted more after I'd kicked her out of my bed the next morning. I knew I was fucked up, but I couldn't help it because someone had fucked with my head, left her mark, and walked away.

Walked away for fucking ever.

When Gavin brought me back to this little beach in North Carolina, I wasn't sure what my plan was. He was worried because we had a new account we were trying to land with a Fortune 500 company. I reassured him I could work from my boat. He knew that, but he'd been worried nonetheless.

Turns out, he was right to worry. I did the bare minimum, we had conference calls when needed, and I did the very least required of me. The rest of the time, I sat on the deck of my boat and watched the world go by, watched summer fade into autumn, the tourists slowly thin, and my mind replayed every single moment Georgia and I had had together this summer.

I thought about getting a dog. Was a boat a place for a dog? I'd seen it plenty of times, but I wasn't interested in a puppy; I wanted a calm, loyal old dog. One that would always be there no matter how much I fucked up. So I went to the local animal shelter and told them what I wanted. An old dog was my only requirement.

They steered me to a sad-looking golden retriever and I knew he was perfect. Charlie was his name. A perfect name to play skipper on my boat.

And Charlie was a perfect boat dog. He livened up a little when I walked him out of the shelter. Our first stop was the pet store for some supplies. He sauntered in somberly, wandered across to a cute little poodle, mounted her, and gave a few half-hearted thrusts. The owner of the perfectly coifed female glared at me as she jerked her dog away. Charlie looked up at me. I shrugged. "I get you. Gotta give it a shot, even if they are out of your league." Charlie wagged his tail once before lifting his leg on the corner of an aisle and pissing on the floor. Fucking fantastic.

So there we were, Charlie and me in the front seat, Sophie blowing up my phone, Gavin worried about where my head was, Drew sending me a text every day, asking how I was doing, and all I could think about was a mass of wild brown hair and a beautiful smile I'd had all summer and had been ripped away from me.

"Whadya say we take a ride, hey, old guy?" I gave Charlie a scratch behind the ears as he sat shotgun with me.

It was my second day with Charlie and we'd just come from town after hitting the bank and post office.

He wagged his tail before he turned and stuck his big head out the window of the passenger side.

I wandered around some back roads on the way home from Wilmington. It was only a Tuesday. I hadn't told Gavin I would be gone, but I didn't have anything important that needed doing in the next handful of hours. I drove and wound my way along deserted, chewed-up roads, headed east toward the coast. I didn't know where I was going, wasn't interested in the GPS on my phone; just knew I'd get to where I needed to be as long as I kept heading east.

Old cottages and fancy beach homes whizzed by the windows. The sea breeze blew through the cab of my battered Jeep Rubicon and tossed my hair onto my forehead. I needed a fucking haircut like three weeks ago. I couldn't stand it in my eyes, but when it came around to actually getting it done, I just never made the time to do it. I ran my fingers through my hair and tried my best to tuck the too-long-but-not-long-enough strands behind my ears with an eye roll. A buzz cut. Maybe I'd get a buzz cut. Got a dog, a boat, and a buzz cut. Hell, maybe I'd even go off the grid. Put the Jeep in storage and sail until I felt like not sailing anymore. Sort of like Forrest Gump when he just went running. Maybe I would just go sailing. My lips pulled down in a frown when I realized I needed a job to make the payments on my boat, and the only job that I was good at was hacking, which required Internet, which required me to live firmly on the grid. There went that idea, then.

"Charlie! Man, fuck you stink. You gotta go to the bathroom, old guy?" Charlie turned and ticked his head to the side before crawling across the console and placing his two front feet on my thigh. I grinned and gave him a pat. I was going to like having a dog. He had the ability to communicate without saying a word. Perfect.

I pulled over on a private stretch of dirt road and climbed out of the vehicle, Charlie bounding out after me. He headed for the underbrush along the ditch and sniffed around, tail wagging the entire time. I leaned against the bumper and watched him with a smile. I shuffled my feet in the dirt and noticed that it was intermixed with sand, making us close to the beach.

"Charlie! Come on, old man, do your business." I hustled him along as he wandered, nose to the ground, farther down the shoulder of the road. He lifted his leg every few feet. "Charlie, come on." I walked along with him and patted him on the flank. He veered into the thicker underbrush off the road and landed at an old sign buried in the ditch. He wagged his tail and sniffed around it. I walked over and bent to find a rusted *For Sale by Owner* sign. I glanced up to find an old two-track trail that led into the woods. Maybe an old cabin was tucked back there; a cabin on the beach. The perfect place to go off the grid, yet not quite. I tipped my head to the sky as my eyes searched for power lines. I needed Internet; I couldn't entertain living anywhere without some Internet to help pay the bills.

"You wanna go for a walk?" I looked up to find Charlie already far out ahead of me on the trail. I glanced back at the Jeep. It was parked far enough off the road, not that this place saw much traffic anyway, so I figured it was safe for a few minutes while I checked out the place that was *For Sale by Owner*.

Charlie and I walked down the two tracks that twisted into the woods. The closer we came to the beach, sand overtook the dirt, before we finally cleared a corner and the old house came into view. My eyes widened for a moment. I clenched my fists at my sides. It couldn't be. No way could it be. I walked around the small cottage, weathered grey shingles and shutters, the roof of the wraparound porch part falling in, and headed for the side of the building. I came around the edge and ducked through the brush before the beach came into view. A long dock cut through the tall grass that waved in the breeze. The dock was in decent shape, considering the state of the house.

I'd seen this dock before. Memories of that night

flashed through my mind. The taste of her skin. The taste of her on my lips. Our mouths tangled together. My hand fisted in her thick hair. Her thighs spread for me. Fuck, how could I have ended up at this house? The place that had been the backdrop for the most beautiful and painful memory of my life? Just one of the memories that had been playing on repeat in my mind. The first night Georgia and I had fucked. Except it had been so much more than that. Way beyond fucking. So far beyond I didn't even have words for it.

I gritted my teeth together and kicked at a leg of the dock.

"Charlie," I hollered and patted my leg to call him. He came bounding out of the woods at full speed, bright eyes, wagging tail, tongue hanging out of his mouth. He looked the liveliest I'd seen him all day. Even more so than when he was trying to stick it in the prissy poodle at the pet store. "Back to the car, old man." I took long strides down the driveway, headed for the road. Fuck me if this didn't serve as some kind of knife in my stomach. Like I hadn't been suffering with the memories enough.

Two

Tristan

The memory of that fucking cottage sat in my mind all week.

And the following week.

I stayed on my boat, dicking around, working here and there, listening to Gavin bitch at me because my head wasn't in the game. I knew he was trying to be patient. I knew he was worried. I got random texts from Drew every few days that were about random stupid shit and I knew they were check-ins. She was worried, possibly more than Gavin was. I think it concerned them that I was alone up here at the scene of the crime with only the memories of Georgia and me surrounding my every thought.

Trouble was, this was the only place I wanted to be. I only wanted to be in the place where we'd made those memories. Hence, the reason that cottage down the shore from her beach house was haunting me. In some fucked-up way, I knew if I had that cottage, I would know if she came back. I realized this made me a full-on stalker. I knew that. I just didn't care.

So I finally dialed the number that had been burned into my brain.

Not only was the place for sale, but also it was well under my budget. Significantly so, probably because the fucking roof looked like it was about to cave in. But I didn't care. I offered the asking price. I think they were desperate to unload the place, as it had sat there abandoned for more than a year. The owner lived out of town and the cottage had belonged to his father, who had passed on. I tried to offer my sympathy, but in reality, I was relieved the place was for sale and was prime location.

I knew I was pathetic.

Wholeheartedly.

I also knew this was a rash decision. Except it felt like it wasn't. I'd tossed it around in my head on the deck of my boat for the better part of two weeks. And the month before that, I'd only thought about this place—about the moments Georgia and I had shared on this beach. If I never saw her again, if she never came back to the beach house and she married Kyle and had her perfect little rug rats and a white picket fence, I wouldn't regret buying the cottage because the summer I'd shared with that one perfect girl had been my perfect summer. Being around her had filled me up inside. So if I never laid eyes on her again, just living with the memory around me would have to be enough, because I knew I had no chance of getting over Georgia Montgomery. Not in this lifetime.

I moved in on a Tuesday. I let the lease run out on my apartment and convinced Gavin to drive a moving truck up with some of my furniture. I paid him in beer. That's all he ever needed. I knew it was unavoidable, but I feared seeing Drew would be torture. She'd driven separately because Gavin would need a way home. I knew she would lay into me the entire few days they were here.

I was right. She did.

I was pissed, but I held it in. That little dark-haired pixie could meddle like no one's business. What punched me in the gut was she spoke to Georgia often; she knew how her life was now. I walked around like a mute, refusing to ask questions, but Drew filled me in anyway.

She told me Georgia was in rough shape.

I told her I didn't care. Secretly, I did. I cared so fucking much it hurt.

Drew told me I should call her. I told her no fucking way. Georgia had to come to me. We'd been a fucking mess all summer, back and forth and back and forth, and I was done with it. Georgia needed to choose me, something she hadn't done all summer.

She also had to choose herself, what *she* wanted. And what she thought she wanted was Kyle, so I had to respect that, no matter how much it made my stomach boil with anger and hurt.

I threw myself on the couch when Gavin and Drew finally left. Back to being by myself, just me and Charlie; exactly how I wanted it. No one to nag me, no one to shoot me pitiful glances. I had my dog, some beer, Internet . . . and it was all I really needed.

One evening, I was at the store picking up more beer and dog food, when I ran into Briana, or was it Kelsey? Fuck if I remembered. I could hardly keep them straight when I'd screwed them this summer. I tossed a jar of peanut butter into my cart when a hand slid around my waist and a husky voice whispered in my ear. I'd be lying if I said my dick didn't twitch to life—purely reactionary—because the second thing my brain registered was this girl was trouble wrapped up in psycho.

"Didn't know you were back in town. Why didn't you call me?" she breathed as her hand trailed down to my ass and gave a squeeze. I rolled my eyes before I turned and plastered a smile on my face.

"Hey, what's up?" I took her in. Briana, I think it was. Tight jeans, heels, bright red sweater that covered her sizable tits, but still managed to be indecent.

"You been here long?" she murmured in my ear as her hand smoothed down the front of my jeans and brushed against my cock. For a split second, I thought about taking her home. My body and mind raged. I wanted to fuck Georgia out of my system. Sink balls-deep into this girl and fuck away the pain. But the thought of being with anyone other than Georgia had my stomach twisting painfully.

"Few weeks," I said before removing her hand from my junk.

"Let's get together. You still have my number, right?" She caressed my arm suggestively.

"Yeah, I have it." That was a lie. I'd cleared all numbers out of my phone that weren't Georgia's one night on the boat when I was drunk and bitter. "I'll call you." I turned back to the cart, trying to blow her off.

"Are you busy tonight? I have plans, but I could be persuaded into canceling them." She brushed her tits against my arm. My dick was still stirring to life. He was all in. My fucking head wasn't, though. I was getting pissed. I was so sick of girls that refused to take a hint.

"Got things to do. Sorry." I pushed the cart down the aisle and headed for the liquor. Tonight was going to be a scotch kind of night.

"Maybe tomorrow, then?" She trailed after me.

"Maybe. I'll call you." I continued to walk.

"Okay, Tristan. Good to see you." She cupped my ass and her fingers wrapped around to my balls from behind. I sucked in a quick breath as all the blood rushed to my dick. My head refused to think straight.

Fuck.

I ground my teeth together.

All I wanted was Georgia.

Could I fuck someone else? Did I want to? I'd tried that all summer and it hadn't worked for shit. Except now, Georgia wasn't here to pull me back in. I wouldn't have to wake up the next morning, the smell of sweaty sex on me from some other chick, and look into her pained eyes. My dick pounded in my jeans as I scrubbed my palm over my face.

"See you later," I grumbled, pushing the cart with a little more force than necessary. I bee-lined for the scotch, grabbed the most expensive bottle they had, and then hit the checkout lane.

Close fucking call. It was a good thing I didn't have the girl's number because it was possible I'd be tempted to cave some night when I was drunk and angry as fuck with Georgia. Thankfully, at this moment, I'd had the foresight to see I'd only wake up with a sick sense of regret in the morning. I headed back out to my truck and prayed I wouldn't run into her again.

Three

Tristan

That week, I finally got back into my routine. I felt semi-settled—my couch, my chair, my TV—I felt like I was getting back to a new normal. I'd hired a contractor to come in and fix up the place, including a new roof. The quaint three-bedroom was small, but I could see the potential. The wide-open space of the kitchen, living, and dining areas made it feel more spacious, and the wraparound deck off the back looked out over the ocean.

Every morning, I woke up just as dawn hit the horizon and went for my morning run with Charlie. He was old, so he dragged ass, but it was good for him to get some exercise. If I let him, he'd lie like a pile of bones on the leather couch all day. He always took his time getting out of the house in the morning, but after a few minutes, we hit a rhythm and he trailed behind me happily.

Despite the fact that we were into late fall and I'd been at the cottage for more than a month now, the days could still have a humid stickiness to them. On those mornings, Charlie and I ran the first half of our morning jog and walked the way back. The dog was odd and had a favorite stick that he kept outside the front door. He chewed on it for a few weeks until it was down to nothing before he'd find another. So it was that morning he'd chosen a new stick and I was tossing it down the beach for him. We were on the way back from our run and he was galloping into the waves, trying to bite at them with his teeth, before I threw the stick and he paddled out to get it. He came bounding back to me, dropped the stick at my feet, and gave a shake *every single fucking time.* Wet dog stink in the morning. Nothing better. I grinned and gave his ears a scratch before throwing the stick back into the water for him. We walked down the beach until my dock and Georgia's beach house came into view. I bit my bottom lip painfully, trying to redirect the pain that sliced into my gut at the sight of her house. I saw the little sand dune where we'd sat and read *Tristan and Iseult.*

Charlie came bounding up to me, dropped the stick, did his shake, and the cool water hitting me brought me out of my thoughts.

"Hey, old man, still got it, don't ya?" I gave him a pat and tossed the stick again, my thoughts returning instantly to Georgia. It'd been over a week since I'd run into Briana at the store and I was thankful I'd turned her down. I was also thankful that I didn't have her number, because I'd gotten so pissed drunk later that night on scotch I probably would have fucked anything on two legs if given the opportunity. In hindsight, scotch had been a bad choice. I was also thankful she didn't know where I lived; I had no doubt she'd be tapping on my door all hours of the night, looking for a fuck if she did. Another Sophie all over again. Christ, was my radar off? Why was I landing in bed with the psycho ones lately?

"Come on, Charlie. Let's head in." I patted my leg and the old dog wagged his tail and then led the way up the dock to the porch of the cottage. I felt a twisting in my stomach, just like I always did when I passed the spot where Georgia and I had had sex for the first time. I kept walking and tried not to go down that road all over again.

The following Saturday afternoon, Charlie and I pulled into the marina, ending what might be our last day on the boat for the season. I locked up the boat before making arrangements with the marina to put it up for the winter. Charlie leaped up into the front seat of the Jeep and I started to make my way back to the cottage before I remembered Charlie needed dog food. I turned the car around and headed for the small pet store in town.

"No humping this time." I pointed a finger at him as we pulled into the parking lot. His tail wagged back and forth as he looked up at me with big, round eyes. "Don't do it, old man. I know you still got it, but you don't have to prove it to every pretty little thing on four legs." He gave a short bark and I smiled. "Come on." I ruffled his ears and then moved aside so he could jump out the driver's side door. I belatedly realized I hadn't put his leash on him, but he was pretty good at sticking by my side and the parking lot was nearly empty this late in the off-season anyway.

Charlie trotted around some cars and out of sight. I rolled my eyes and followed him around the back end of a car.

"Charlie!" I rounded the bumper. "Charlie, come on." I slapped my thigh to get his attention.

"Tristan," a soft voice carried on the wind. I lifted my eyes from his wagging tail and saw a dark mane of chestnut hair cascading around his big dog head and gorgeous brown eyes that had been keeping me awake at night peering back at me.

"Georgia?" Was I seeing things? Was she really here, stooped over in a parking lot, petting my dog? The girl who'd consumed my thoughts the past three fucking months. Had I wished her into existence? Was I going insane? "What are you doing here?" I asked, my mind a whirlwind of emotion—confusion, anger, and pain the most prominent three.

"I came back," was her simple answer. What did she mean she *came back*? Was she here to stay? Was there a problem? Had Kyle done something to her and she was running? I knew I didn't trust the guy the moment I'd laid eyes on him. The way he acted around her—as if he owned her, talked down to her—made my stomach crawl.

"To the beach house? When?" I squatted and patted Charlie as I spoke.

"Beginning of November."

My mind computed the time.

Over a month?

She'd been right under my nose for over a month and I hadn't noticed?

I searched my memory for a sign she'd been at the beach house, something I'd missed, but I found none. Maybe I hadn't been paying attention. Maybe I'd been walking around in a drunken stupor too much of the time to see the girl I wanted so desperately right next door.

Anger boiled in my stomach.

She'd left me.

She'd lied and said she'd be back, then she hadn't even picked up her phone. I was so bitter, so angry that this girl who'd consumed me all fucking summer was back. I wanted to hold onto the anger—she'd proven why I'd hit the road at any sign of commitment in the past; women had the ability to suck you in, like a siren call, and then walk away without another glance back. I'd learned that lesson the instant my mom had left and my dad had spiraled into his dark place.

What pissed me off even more than seeing her standing in front of me, looking so beautiful and serene, was a sliver of hope in my heart that we could be *us* again. I wanted her but I didn't *want* to want her. I wanted to hold onto the anger and pain and blame her, because being numb was easier than opening up.

"You've been here for more than a month?" I asked numbly.

"Yeah. I've been fixing up the place for winter."

"You're staying? Permanently? What about Kyle? Is he here?" I took a quick glance around the parking lot. I was as good as gone if he was here. I was sure I'd sock him in the jaw if I ever saw his face again, just for the mere fact that she'd chosen him, been sharing his bed since August.

"I'm staying, hopefully forever. I don't think anything could pull me away from here, not anymore. And Kyle isn't with me." She frowned before she finished. "We're, not really . . . together."

What? Suddenly rage boiled inside me. Why hadn't she

called me? I'd come to terms that she'd chosen Kyle in August, but she was back; she'd left him. So why hadn't she called?

Because she doesn't want you. Just because she finally walked away from him, doesn't mean she's choosing you. What could you give her? Heartache? A tainted past? She deserves so much better.

She did. I knew it.

I stayed silent as the pain radiated through my body.

"What about you? Why are you here? And whose dog is this? Oh God, are you with Briana or Kelsey or whoever?" I watched her eyes take in the parking lot, looking for someone.

"The slut parade?" An amused smile lit my lips at the term she'd coined this summer. "No, I haven't seen them since I've been back." That was a lie, but only a white one. I wished I'd never seen Briana that night in the grocery store, and it hadn't led anywhere anyway, so no point in letting Georgia's mind travel that path.

I straightened my legs and watched her stand across from me. My eyes took in her face like I was starved for her beauty, because I was.

Completely.

I'd gone without her for nearly three months. Three months without a single word.

I wanted to take her in, soak her up, and take a piece of her with me when I left because I knew just because she was here, and I was here, didn't mean she would choose me. But if there was one thing I wanted her to know it was this: I would fucking choose her. I would always choose her.

"How long have you been back?" Her dark chocolate eyes swirled with emotion.

"I never really left, I guess." I couldn't tear my eyes from hers.

"What? Since the hurricane?" Confusion flashed across her face. Shit, I knew how this made me look. Like a pathetic stalker. Well, too bad, because I was. I came back because I couldn't leave. There, I'd admitted it. I'd come because if I couldn't be with her, I wanted to be in the place we'd been together.

"Well, I went back to Jacksonville and when the hurricane cleared out a few days later, Gavin drove me back to get the boat. But when I got here, I couldn't leave again." *I couldn't leave because of you, Georgia. Are you getting that?* "I stayed on my boat for a while until I managed to work something else out."

"You moved here?"

"I bought a house, Georgia."

Her eyes narrowed on me.

"I bought the cottage. Down the beach . . ." I could see

it all coming together for her. I could see her eyes blazing with recognition. The realization that I'd come back for her.

"The cottage? The dog, the stranger—that was you?" she murmured.

"Umm . . . not sure where you're going with that . . ." A smile lifted the corner of my lips. Her eyes flickered down to my mouth and stayed there.

God, she was still affected. My heart hammered in my chest and I yearned to reach out and take her in my arms. Emotion flooded my brain because I'd fucking dreamed of holding her again for three long goddamn months.

Get it together, man. Don't fall apart. Cool and calm. Don't ruin this. Even if she wants to just be friends, you need her in your life.

But what if she didn't want that? The evil little guy on my shoulder taunted me. What if she never wanted me in her life again? Could I deal with her living down the beach from me and never see her? Jesus, that would kill me. This girl had the ability to lay me open and she didn't have any idea.

"A few weeks ago, I saw someone walking a dog, and they went into the cottage. That was you?"

"I take Charlie for a walk every morning." I gave Charlie a scratch behind the ears because I needed the distraction. If I was going to try to remain calm and cool, I needed a distraction from her sweet, heart-shaped face staring back at me.

"You bought the cottage?"

"Our cottage? Yeah." Fuck, there I said it. Our cottage. Because it was our cottage. It was the way I'd been thinking of it from the moment I'd walked down the driveway and saw it open up before me.

"I can't believe you were right there," she muttered.

"And you were too." I wondered how things would have gone if we'd run into each other a month ago. Would we be together now? Would we ever again? Would she let me in?

Then the sky opened up above us and she squinted her eyes in the most adorable way, so adorable my heart tore open and I knew this was it, but I couldn't let it be. I couldn't let her walk away again. I was scared shitless she'd turn me away. A squeal escaped her throat as the rain poured down harder and she dodged around her car to land in her front seat. I stood, my hands stuffed in the pockets of my jeans, shoulders hunched, drowning like a street rat with the biggest smile on my face because she looked happy. So fucking happy for the first time since the early part of the summer. I'd stand in this fucking rainstorm and watch her all day as long as that smile lit her cheeks.

"Dinner?" she called out to me.

My eyebrows shot up in surprise; my heart thudded in my chest. "When?" I took a step closer.

"Tonight. Manicotti?" A warm smile spread across her face.

Manicotti. My mind shot right back to the first day we'd met so many months ago. Little did I know this girl would find some long-forgotten corner inside my heart and crawl into it. Imprint herself on my soul and refuse to leave. "You Italian or something?" I grinned as cold rain streamed down my face. She watched me for a few moments before she opened her car door, stood, and walked to me slowly. My eyes narrowed in confusion.

She finally reached me, our chests just a hair's breadth apart, my heart thudding in my chest, wondering what her next move would be. A soft smile lifted her cheeks as she brought her hand up, her fingertips dusting along my forehead, moving wet strands out of my eyes. My heart leaped into my throat and a smile spread across my face.

She brought her other hand up to cup my cheek as she leaned in ever so slowly, her lips searching out mine. Finally, we connected. Our lips pressed together, not moving, just relishing the long, overdue connection. I couldn't stand the distance that was left between us any longer. I needed my hands on her. To feel her, to know she was here and real. I lifted my palms and held her heartbreakingly beautiful face, the pads of my thumbs caressing her cheekbones. My lips began to move against hers slowly, relishing her taste, the feel of her skin against mine. I lost myself in her scent, her lips, her touch as her fingers ran through my wet hair. Pleasure rippled through my body—happiness and bliss erupting. My heart pounded in my ears. It felt like it would crack a hole straight through my chest. She was here. My beautiful, dark-haired girl was here and she was back. I just prayed to God that this meant she was choosing me.

Four

Tristan

I ran into the pet store to grab Charlie some food and to collect myself. I told Georgia I'd meet her at her place just as soon as I was done. My mind reeled with the possibility. Did this mean something for us? Or was this just two friends catching up? I was so anxious to lay my eyes on her face again.

Her beautiful, soft brown eyes.

She'd seemed guarded when she first saw me, but there was an unmistakable sparkle. I felt in my bones that she'd thought of me too while we'd been apart. She seemed happy, and yet she wasn't with Kyle.

I coaxed Charlie into the Jeep, then ran back into the grocery store she'd just been in, the place I'd run into Briana a few weeks before. I grabbed a bottle of the most expensive wine I could find from the vineyard we'd visited up the coast last summer. I got behind the wheel of the Jeep, and suddenly my stomach was twisting with nerves to see her again. I couldn't stay away. I wouldn't survive if she pushed me away again.

I knocked lightly before crossing the threshold of the beach house into the delicious, homey aroma of Italian cooking. My eyes scanned the living room, the dining room, and finally, the kitchen before they landed on her. I drank her in. Her entire form. She turned to me, a smile on her face. I stepped closer to her, my eyes trained on her chocolate-colored depths. I was unwilling to break the contact for which I'd been starved for months. I wanted her lips pressed to mine again—my hands holding her face, but I was fucking terrified. Terrified to push her too far. Maybe that had been why she'd run from me all summer: I'd laid my cards on the table with her at every chance and I'd scared her off.

I'd never had an issue with women before, but here I was second guessing every single thought I had about this girl. I wanted desperately to go with my gut, but my gut had been wrong about her much of the time.

I stepped into the kitchen and her smile widened. My lips quirked up in a flirty grin.

"Smells great," I mumbled. It did smell great, but the food was the furthest thing from my mind.

"Thanks. Wine?" She nodded at the bottle in my hand.

"Yeah, from Tabor Hill." I set the bottle on the counter. She turned and stretched up on her tiptoes to reach for the goblets on the top shelf. Her lightweight sweater inched up her waist, revealing a flash of skin, hugging the smooth curves of her form. I pressed my lips together, trying to hold in the tortured groan that landed in my throat. Just like that first day we'd met, except then she'd been in shorts and a tiny tank top, long, shapely legs stretching high. I think I had audibly groaned that day, and I was barely containing it today.

"Can you open it?" she murmured as she turned back to me, her eyes boring into mine. We were running through the motions, but the last thing on each of our minds, I thought, was the wine.

"Of course." I stood in place, not bothering to grab the corkscrew from the drawer. She stepped closer and set the glasses on the counter next to the bottle. We stood a few inches apart and her scent invaded my space. My blood hummed with need for her. All of her. I wanted desperately to have my hands on her skin.

"Georgia." I lifted a hand to cup her cheek. My thumb ran up her cheekbone and her eyes fluttered closed as she leaned into my touch. My heartbeat roared in my chest as I committed her sweet face to my memory. It was so much fucking better than I'd remembered. How I'd survived without being in her presence, I didn't know. But in reality, I hadn't survived, not at all. I'd been a drunken idiot who'd let every other important thing in my life fall away.

"It's great to see you," I said, barely above a whisper. They were the only words that I could form, but so many more swirled in my head. Words I didn't even want to consider. All I knew was in this moment, I felt whole again. This girl filled something up in me I didn't understand; something I never thought possible and something I didn't realize was necessary for me to thrive, but there it was. Georgia was here and I couldn't have been happier.

Her eyes flickered open and bore into mine. She looked like she was searching for answers before she cleared her throat and turned back to the stove. "Five minutes until it's done." She pulled plates and silverware out of drawers and set them on the island. I swallowed the lump in my throat at the prospect of sitting next to her, as opposed to across from her at the dining room table. My nerve endings tingled, my dick stirred to life at the prospect of feeling her skin on mine, rolling in bed with her, her thick dark hair laid out on the pillow beneath me.

I cleared my throat and tried to get my thoughts under control as I opened the wine and set the bottle near our plates to breathe. She busied herself around the kitchen. The room fell silent.

It was awkward.

And perfect.

Both in the same breath.

I didn't know it was possible, but just being in her presence calmed me. She was fucking here and I was devising ways to have her never leave me again. Should I lock her up and keep her in my house like a caveman? Handcuff her to my bedpost and ravage her soft body whenever it pleased me? A smile tilted my lips at the thought. It sounded like a fucking dream. A fantasy come to life—ravaging Georgia whenever, wherever.

"It's ready," she said softly at my side as she laid the steaming dish of manicotti on the island. We each made our way around opposite ends and sat at the barstools. I poured wine into our glasses. She lifted the goblet to her sweet lips and took a swallow. I watched her throat move and contract and I instantly wanted to wrap my hand around her neck and bite and lick and claim her.

Without thinking, I snaked my hand over to her thigh and rested it there. Her eyes darted down to my hand holding her denim-covered leg. I gave it a soft squeeze and sucked my bottom lip between my teeth, watching her, begging with every fiber in me that she wouldn't push me away. My heart couldn't fucking handle it if she pushed me away again. Her eyes lifted to meet mine as her lips parted, sucking in a slow breath.

"Tristan." My name escaped her lips in a whisper.

I shut her down before she could say more. I wasn't prepared for what she might tell me. "Thanks for inviting me to dinner." I grinned that easy grin that I reserved only for women and then pulled my hand away, dishing manicotti out for both of us.

Five

Tristan

A week went by in no time at all. Every morning, I walked Charlie down the beach and, on the way back, I gave Georgia a wave as she sat on the deck, sipping her coffee. Every morning, I wanted to run to her. I wanted her to run to me. I wanted her in my bed because she was already consuming my thoughts, but I was restraining myself. I had to try. Restraining myself was the last thing I'd done all summer. I'd let my impulsive emotions get the best of me and it hadn't worked, so now I was taking it slow. I was doing what I should have done all summer. I was letting her come to the realization that she wanted me too. It was taking longer than I expected—I wasn't used to waiting on a girl—but I was determined to make it work, because if it didn't, I would go crazy.

She finally called the following week. I was waiting for her call, wondering how long it would take, pulling my hair out waiting for it. But finally, it came.

"Dinner?" she chirped over the line. I glanced up at the clock and noted it was after five.

"What's on the menu?" I grinned as I pretended to consider her offer. Like there was a chance in hell I would be turning her down.

"Chili. It's been simmering in the slow cooker all day and I have tons. I thought it only neighborly to share." I could hear the smile in her voice.

"Definitely the neighborly thing to do." And much more. If this girl were just my neighbor, my dick wouldn't be twitching in my pants right now. "What time?" I asked as I adjusted myself to ease the ache at the sound of her voice.

"Now?"

"Not one for scheduling, huh?" I huffed as a smile tipped my lips at the idea of seeing her again.

"We can do it another time . . ." she trailed off softly. Was that disappointment in her voice? Fuck, I hoped so.

"No, I'll be down in five."

"Bring Charlie too. I have something for him," she said before hanging up. I wrinkled my forehead. She had something for my dog? Charlie was higher up on her list than I was? Not that I wanted something from her—I wanted everything. Anything she would give me. I had to do something to move this dance along faster. My brain warred with itself, wondering if I could wait her out or beg her to have me like that pathetic fool I was.

After brushing my teeth and running a hand through my hopeless mop of hair that for some reason had women dropping their panties and falling into my bed, I called for Charlie and headed out the door and down the beach. I jogged up her deck, Charlie on my heels, and tapped on the French doors before stepping in. Georgia looked up at me, a smile spread across her sweet face as she set the table.

She took my breath away.

My eyes burned with need for her and my mouth lifted in a wide grin, as I found myself doing only when she was around.

Her dark brown hair fell in a cascade of waves over one shoulder. She wore an oversized sweater and dark leggings. And she was barefoot. Breathtaking and barefoot. She looked so at home, such a domestic picture, I knew it would punch me straight in the heart if I couldn't see her every day for the rest of my life.

The silence stretched between us as I continued to grin at her, taking in her beautiful form. Her cheeks pinked up and the smile fell from her lips for a moment.

"Everything okay?" She tipped her head at me.

I cleared my throat. "Yeah." I took the few remaining steps toward her, invading her space, inhaling her scent. I reached a hand up to twist a thick lock of her dark hair between my fingers. The strands were silky and slid against my skin. She sucked in a quick breath and her eyes held mine, questions swirling. "You look beautiful," I murmured.

"Oh." Her mouth formed an O in the most adorable way. "Thank you."

I nodded, my eyes scorching into hers before I finally dropped my hand. I swallowed and willed myself to keep control. I could ravage her right across this table. Lay her out, listen to her moan in my ear, her legs around my hips. Fuck, I missed my hands on her body. "Need help with anything?" I turned toward the kitchen and tried my best to adjust myself discreetly. I wasn't sure if it was more painful not having her in my life, or seeing her occasionally, knowing she was just down the beach and I couldn't touch her.

"Charlie's gift," Georgia shrieked and launched herself off the couch, heading down the hallway. I chuckled as I watched her retreating form. We'd finished the best chili I'd ever had, and were now each two beers in and settled on the couch. We were laughing and talking and she was giggling in the most delightful fashion. I was trying desperately to control my raging need for this beautiful girl.

"Why does Charlie get a gift and I'm left high and dry?" A flirty smile lit my face when she walked back in with an oversized, basting bone.

"Who says you're getting left high and dry?"

My eyebrows shot up into my hairline as I watched her eyes sparkle with flirtatious amusement. I was dumbfounded. She was flirting with me. We hadn't shared a single fucking touch since that kiss in the parking lot at the grocery store nearly a week ago and she was finally flirting with me. Had I finally broken her resolve? Had I been right to wait her out and not push her?

Regardless, I couldn't form words as I watched her bend down and call Charlie to her. She scratched his ears and patted his head lovingly before passing him the bone. He wagged his tail and then sauntered off proudly, settling himself in the corner to gnaw on his prize.

My eyes followed her as she came to sit on the couch next to me. She turned, her body facing mine, one leg drawn up and tucked underneath the other. I chewed on my bottom lip as she took another swallow of her beer.

"Why did you leave?" I blurted. Fuck! Why had I said that? I hadn't meant to get into serious topics, hadn't ever meant to get into the past with her. I wanted to leave all of that shit right where it belonged.

She coughed for a moment in surprise before setting the beer bottle down. "I . . . I don't . . . it wasn't . . ." she stammered, looking for an explanation.

"Sorry. I didn't mean to bring it up. You don't have to answer. It's just something I've wondered about—if you knew you weren't coming back. And then when I called and you never . . ." I trailed off and ripped my gaze from hers.

"It's okay. I guess I owe you an explanation." She drew her bottom lip between her teeth and began gnawing on the pink flesh fiercely. "I don't want to rehash things that have already been said. It's terrible, all of the decisions I made during the summer. I have so many regrets."

Regrets.

There was that word. We'd promised each other no regrets, so was she telling me she regretted me? All of it? Because I sure as hell didn't. She was the last thing I regretted. I regretted I'd tried my stupid caveman way of forgetting her by fucking other girls and flaunting it. I regretted it so much the bile rose in my throat at the memory of the pain etched across her face.

But, her? I didn't regret her.

And if she told me she regretted me, I didn't know what I would do. But I knew it would include a bottle of scotch.

"I think I wanted to come back. I left a piece of myself here. The biggest piece. I left *me* here. But when I got back to DC, I just . . . was consumed by Kyle. He's like that; takes over my whole world . . . we always go back to each other."

"Is this time different?" I asked her point-blank. I had to know.

Her brows furrowed as she took in my words. "Yes," she said. I watched for any indication that she didn't believe what she was saying. I didn't see any. She looked determined. Her jaw set, her eyes hard.

"Do you think that means something for us?" I didn't want to ask it, but I wanted it answered. I was trying not to lay my cards on the table, but that's who I am. I don't pull bullshit. I don't play games. I'm straightforward and what I needed at that moment was to know what she was thinking about us.

"Tristan," she murmured, her eyes downcast, still chewing on her lip.

"Sorry, don't answer. I didn't mean to get into all of this. I'm just here for dinner." I shot her my best reassuring smile, but it didn't seem to help. She was still lost in thought, playing with the label on her beer bottle.

"Hey." I scooted closer to her on the couch and rested my palm on her knee. Her eyes darted up to meet mine, emotions swirling, unanswered questions burning. I ran my thumb along the soft fabric of her leggings and watched her breathing pick up, her chest heaving as her lips parted and she inhaled deeply.

"I want us . . . I want to be . . ." She hardened the set of her jaw and glanced away from me.

She wants what?

She wants us to be friends?

Fuck, please don't let her say she just wants to be friends. I glanced at Charlie and mentally willed him to prepare for a hasty exit, but his old brown eyes refused to meet mine. Distracted fucker. Give him a bone and he's rendered useless. Fuck him. I'll leave him. If she says she just wants to be friends, I'm out the door in a flash, no turning back.

"I want you, but more than that, I want to take it slow," she said on a rush of breath. I was so lost in my thoughts it took a moment for my brain to register her words.

She wants me.

Holy fuck, Georgia wants me.

The one thing I'd been desperate for her to say all summer and she'd just said it.

I heaved a giant sigh and the anxiety that had settled in my chest eased. I clenched my eyes tightly and ran my palm over my face.

"I . . . do you not want that?" she squeaked. I scrubbed my palm across my face and then met her eyes, a grin breaking out across my mouth. I was so fucking relieved. A weight had lifted from my shoulders.

"I can give you slow, Georgia. I don't know if I can give you space, because the last five days have been torture having you right here and not seeing you, but I'll give you slow. Just don't ask me to stay away." I leaned into her, fisted one hand in her thick hair and pulled her lips to mine. I claimed her in a fierce kiss—strong, confident, quick—and then pulled away again.

Her eyes were wide with shock. Her breath came out in quick pants.

She was so fucking turned on it was evident by that hooded look in her eyes, her chest rising and falling, the way she shifted her legs. Fuck yes, I had her. I could work with this. If she wanted it slow, we could take it slow, but that didn't mean I was not going to torture her every step of the way. I threw her a lopsided grin and then lifted the beer bottle to my lips, swallowing the cold liquid and watching her fuss with her hair and averting her eyes from mine. Georgia was mine, whether she knew it or not. This was our new beginning.

Six

Tristan

A few weeks into taking it slow and things were perfect, or as perfect as they could be without having her in my bed every night. But nearly just as good was seeing her beautiful smile over dinner each night and having coffee together every morning, just like we had every day last summer.

That night after we, or she, had decided to take it slow, she'd insisted on getting a tour of my cottage. So much had happened to us there. One night at the end of the dock in the sand, and it had changed my world forever. Yet she'd never been inside the place. So I held her hand as we wandered down the beach, Charlie trotting happily in front of us.

We walked up the boardwalk and avoided the uncomfortable silence that stretched between us when we passed the end where we'd shared our first moment this past summer. I laid my hand on her back when she stepped over the threshold, being the perfect gentleman I thought I was, and then she busted down into a fit of giggles. She'd finally admitted there was no way she was taking another step into this house until it had a fresh coat of paint and some fixing up.

Two weeks later, she was putting me to work. Saturday morning, bright and early, I was near salivating as she was tramping through my door: hair in a messy knot on the top of her head, yoga pants hugging the curve of her ass perfectly, and paint rollers in hand. She'd sent me to pick up cans of paint the night before and, because I had zero concern for style, I'd let her pick out the paint color.

She'd insisted it be a surprise.

And was it ever when I lifted the lid. "This is pink." I narrowed my eyes.

"It's not pink. It's salmon." She grinned as she set up the paint trays.

"Not putting pink on my walls."

"Salmon, and you are. I seem to recall you relinquishing control of this decision." She arched an eyebrow at me.

"There was an unspoken understanding there would be no pink."

"Salmon." She stood, hands on her hips, and faced me.

"Fucking pink. And it's not going on my walls."

She shot me a nasty look before stepping closer. We

stood head to head and determination flared in her eyes. It was so fucking hot, I had to adjust myself. Fuck discretion. Her eyes flickered down at the movement before her gaze met mine again, a smirk playing on her lips.

She leaned in close to me, one hand threading in my hair, her lips dusting along my jaw, her breath whispering in my ear. "It's salmon, and if you know what's good for you, you're going to help me *lay* it on your walls." She gave a tug before turning and bending over to pour paint in the tray.

I heaved an exasperated sigh as my eyes took in her long legs, her ass facing me, bent at the waist.

"Vixen."

She giggled and shot me a grin around her back. She knew exactly what she was doing.

"You wanna play that game, baby?" I stepped up behind her and brushed my hips lightly against her ass. I trailed a hand down the expanse of her back, feeling each and every dip and curve in her spine. Finally, my hand trailed across the curve of her bottom and I grabbed both of her hips in my hands and pulled her harder into me. I rotated my hips suggestively, my cock running the length of her cheeks. It felt so fucking good to relieve the pent up pressure. She moaned and rocked softly back into me.

My eyes fluttered closed and I relished her body pressed

tightly to mine before running my hand up and underneath her shirt to connect with her skin. I pressed my fingertips into her spine and worked my way up her back before moving down again to land at the hollow.

So fucking soft. Sweet. Intoxicating. She had me in every way there was to be had.

"Tristan," she moaned my name and my brain fogged up with lust. I gritted my teeth together as my dick begged me to ram into her at full force, while my head reminded me that she'd wanted to take it slow.

But my dick argued that we had been taking it slow. *Very* fucking slow.

But Georgia needed to be in control of the dance we had been doing the last few weeks.

She'd never been in control of her life until now, so I wasn't about to take that away from her. My fingertips dug into the soft flesh at her hips before I dragged my body away from hers.

I stepped back and ran my palm over my face and through my hair, giving it a frustrated tug.

"Fuck," she whispered as she bent at the knees and supported herself on a hand on the floor.

"Yeah," I murmured. "I need a shower."

"Me too." She stood and sucked in a quick breath to catch her bearings.

"Georgia," I groaned. "You can't say shit like that." I gritted my teeth together and clenched my fist in my hair.

"Sorry." She frowned, but a flirty glint lit her eyes.

Such a vixen.

"You need a minute? Or can we get on with it?" She tilted her head with a flirty grin. I wanted desperately to tell her I was so ready to get on with it: in my bed, on the floor, against the wall, in the shower. Definitely in the shower—rivulets of water streaming down her body, the curve of her breasts, the dip of her hips.

I huffed in exasperation. "So, pink . . . salmon . . . it is." I lifted a roller in defeat.

"I thought you'd see it my way." She grinned and turned back to the paint tray.

"You seduced me," I mumbled before dragging the roller through the fresh paint and putting the first lick of pink on the wall.

I glanced around the room and took in the bright paint color she'd insisted on putting on my walls. Last time I relinquished power to this vixen *ever*. It looked good, brighter than I would have picked, and striking against the white trim of the house.

Georgia and I curled up on my couch, watching an old movie. Well, she was watching; I was busy snuggling into her hair and inhaling her vanilla scent, which drove me to distraction. I was also trying like hell to keep from distracting her with my hard-on. It was torture, being pressed to the curve of her body, but it was the sweetest torture imaginable. I wouldn't have wanted to be anywhere else. I slid my hand down her torso, my fingertips stroking dangerously close to the swell of her breast.

"Hey," she murmured and pushed my hand away.

"Can't blame me." I nuzzled deeper into her ear and snagged her earlobe with my teeth.

"We're taking it slow," she reminded me.

"Tortuously slow," I groaned into her ear.

"Calm your raging sexual appetite." She squirmed in my arms and made the torture that much more unbearable.

"Impossible when you're in the room."

"Try harder," she whimpered when I skimmed my hand up her stomach and brushed the underside of her breast with my thumb. My brain fogged over as a moan escaped her throat. She rolled over into me and I adjusted myself, relaxing on my elbow, hovering above her delicious form. My other hand slid up to cup the soft flesh of her neck, my thumb whispering along her jaw. Her eyes fluttered closed as her breathing picked up, her chest heaving.

This was it. Could I have her? Right now? Could I drive her to the point of no return?

Maybe.

Did she want it? Right now? Was she ready?

"Georgia," I murmured in her ear.

"Hmm?" she answered softly as she pressed her soft body into mine.

"Spend Thanksgiving in Jacksonville with me." I flicked her earlobe with my tongue. She froze in place, her breathing halted, before her eyes opened. Her eyebrows scrunched together.

"You want me to come home with you?"

"Yeah."

I watched the thoughts fly through her brain. I knew she was dissecting my words, trying to figure out what they meant. What it meant if she said yes.

"Okay," she finally relented, a small smile lifting her lips.

"Okay," I repeated before brushing my thumb along her full, lower lip. I bent down and touched it with my own lips in a soft kiss. I kissed from corner to corner, rubbing her jaw line gently with my thumb before I pressed a little harder, needier, asking for more. She wrapped her arms around my neck and pressed her body into mine, her tongue licked my bottom lip, asking for entry. I opened and our tongues worked together languidly. I reached a hand up and under her sweater and caressed the soft skin at her hip and around her waist. I teased and nipped at her lips, relishing the satin of her skin under my fingertips. She threaded both hands in my hair and urgently pulled my head closer.

She was saying yes. She wanted more. She moaned and writhed underneath me, like I'd been dreaming the past few months. We'd taken things slowly. We'd been hanging out for a few weeks and this was the furthest we'd gotten. I was painfully hard as I thrust my hips into her, dry humping her on the couch like a teenager.

I groaned and sucked her lower lip between my own as I pulled away. She was going to have to work harder than this.

"Taking it slow, remember?" I pulled away and flashed her that lopsided grin that left her eyes hooded with lust. She narrowed her browns at me and a scowl crossed her face.

"Right." She pushed herself up from couch and landed a palm on my chest, pushing me back from her. I grinned wider because she was so cute when she was angry and sexually frustrated.

"Your terms." I shrugged one shoulder and settled back in the couch.

"Yep," she murmured as she straightened herself out.

Seven

Tristan

"I'm nervous." Georgia bounced in the seat of my Jeep. It was two days before Thanksgiving and we were just a few short blocks from my childhood home.

"Don't be. My dad's laid back."

"But what if I screw up the turkey? What if he doesn't like my pumpkin pie? So much to live up to," she moaned next to me.

"Most holidays, we eat out, so this will be a monumental step up." I clasped her knee to prevent her from shaking it.

"Charlie's nervous too. All that panting, huh, boy?" She turned and gave my dog a scratch behind his ears and a nuzzle into the fur of his neck. He licked across her cheek and she giggled. It was the best noise I'd ever heard.

"His breath is about to knock me out," I complained.

"Shh, he can hear, ya know." She covered both of his

ears with her hands. I rolled my eyes at her as the grin spread across my lips. So adorably fucking cute.

Her phone dinged with a text. She fished it out of her purse as I watched her out of the corner of my eye. A frown marred her beautiful face and she sucked her lip between her teeth. I pulled into the driveway of the small, suburban Cape Cod where I'd grown up.

“Everything okay?” I rubbed her thigh with my hand, hoping to ease the worry on her face.

Her eyes darted to mine and a bevy of emotions flicked through their brown depths. “Yeah.” She tried her best to fake a smile, but I could read right through it. “Let’s go. I can’t wait to meet your dad.” She hopped out of the car. I stood up and narrowed my eyes at her. She was definitely hiding something, but her eyes avoided mine as she shuffled through her big-ass purse for something. I let Charlie out of the backseat and made my way around the car to her.

I rested a hand on her lower back. “You sure everything's okay?” I dipped my head to catch her eyes with mine.

“Mhmm,” she hummed without meeting my eyes. I heaved a sigh and grabbed both of our bags before escorting her into the house.

The next morning, Georgia's alarm went off much earlier than any sane person should ever get up and she hauled my ass out of bed to start the turkey. We were sharing a bed at my dad's house, but that's all we were doing. My dad had told embarrassing stories the night before—he was always chatty when company was over; too chatty for my liking. He regaled Georgia with stories of when I was eight and fell out of a tree and had to get my arm casted. And when I goosed the babysitter when I was eleven and was forced to apologize. She'd laughed hysterically at that and I'd only shrugged. The sexual prowess that had rolled off me from a young age couldn't be contained. She'd socked me in the shoulder for that one and before she could lean away, I'd pressed her lips to mine in a kiss. She froze and then shoved me away with an indulgent smile.

So here I was at four in the morning, basting a turkey while Georgia fluttered around me. How could she be so fucking awake at this hour? I was dragging ass all over the place. Finally, she leaned down and slid the bird into the oven. On her way back up, I wrapped my arms around her waist and skimmed my nose along the line of her neck.

"Back to bed," I murmured.

"We have to be up in a few hours to baste again." She wrapped her arms around my own, which were locked at her waist.

"I just want you to myself today."

"Can't leave people hungry on Thanksgiving." I heard the smile in her voice.

"I won't go hungry." I thrust my hips into her ass and nipped at the flesh of her neck.

"You are relentless," she murmured as she turned in my arms and pressed her lips to mine. I kissed her and ran my hands up her back, pressing her body into mine, feeling every curve and dip.

"I wish you were naked right now," I murmured against her lips.

"You're a hornball," she mumbled between kisses.

"Your fault for making me wait. It's torture not being inside you," I muttered.

I heard her breath hitch at my words. "You wouldn't in your dad's kitchen."

"I definitely *would* in my dad's kitchen." I eased her back against the counter and captured her lips with mine. She wove her fingers in my hair as our tongues tangled together.

"Bedroom." She finally pulled away. I lifted her into my arms and she wrapped her legs around my hips without a word. I carried her down the hall and laid her out on the bed beneath me before pressing her lips to my own and thrusting my hips against hers. So fucking soft and smooth, her scent surrounding me, her hair fanned out on the white sheets—I wanted her so fucking bad, I couldn't see straight.

"Can I have a minute?" She pulled away.

"Okay." I watched her as she gave me one last peck and crawled out from beneath me. She trotted to the bathroom and I lay back on the bed to wait for her. I was so keyed up, my bloodstream hummed with need for her. I didn't know how much longer I could take things slow. I was just hoping she would break soon because if she didn't, I would. There was only so much a man could take, and I knew what it felt like to be buried inside her.

I fucking needed it.

I needed her.

I groaned and tossed my arm over my eyes as I waited. If she didn't hurry up, I would need to take things into my own hands, which probably wouldn't be a bad idea, considering I would probably be a two-pump chump when I finally was deep inside her again. I settled back into the pillow and waited.

"You should have woken me up." I smacked her on the ass as she was setting the table later that day. Dad was plopped in front of the TV watching football, and Georgia and I were getting together the last few things for dinner.

"You looked so peaceful, and I figured if you'd fallen asleep . . ." she murmured and pecked me on the lips chastely. I groaned. I'd fallen a-fucking-sleep waiting for her to come out of the bathroom in the wee hours of the morning after she'd woken me up to baste the turkey and given me a raging hard-on.

"Baby, next time . . . Wake. Me. Up." I glared at her. She only giggled before spinning around and grabbing a few more dishes to set at the table. The doorbell rang and I shot a look to my dad from the kitchen. His eyes still were trained on the game; apparently, he hadn't heard or he was ignoring it.

"Expecting company?" I said as I sauntered by him toward the door.

"Nope," he answered. I opened the door and a female barreled into my arms and wrapped herself around me, head to toe.

"Sasha," I muttered as I breathed in her familiar scent. Lavender. Her mom grew lavender and always had it hanging in the house.

Sasha and I had grown up together; she'd moved in next door when I was a kid and we'd been inseparable. Her mom sort of took my dad and me under her wing. Sasha's dad had left her, and her sister and mom, when she was little. I think her mom secretly had a crush on my dad, the way she doted over him and made his favorite meals, but he seemed blind to any attention she'd paid to him.

"How are you?" she squealed and pulled away, her hands resting on my shoulders.

"I'm great." A wide smile spread across my face. "It's good to see you. Been a long time."

"I saw your Jeep in the driveway and had to pop over to say hi. Am I interrupting?" She ducked her head around me. "Hey, Mr. Howell."

"Sasha! Come in. Tristan, invite her in for Christ's sake." He ambled over and shoved me aside before wrapping her in his arms. "Where's your mom?" He glanced over her shoulder. Maybe hadn't been so unaware of her attention after all.

"Her and my stepdad went on a cruise, so it's just me."

My dad's face fell a little. "Right. Join us for dinner then. It's just about done."

"No, it's all right. I just wanted to say hi." Her eyes searched out mine again. She looked great. Bronze skin and dark, nearly black hair that lent her face an exotic look.

"No, join us; we have plenty of food."

"You sure? I've been in Korea, teaching for the last year. I missed every holiday, and then Mom and Bob went away . . ." she trailed off.

"We'd love to have you." Dad slung an arm over her shoulder and pulled her into the house. The three of us walked into the dining room to find Georgia just setting the turkey down at the table.

"Hi." Georgia's eyes flickered with confusion. Fuck, was this going to be complicated?

"I'm Sasha. Tristan and I grew up together." She knocked me in the shoulder with a playful smile.

"I'm Georgia. Tristan's . . . friend." Georgia averted her eyes from mine. Fuck, I should have introduced them. I could feel the tension racketing around the room, Georgia's unanswered questions clear in her eyes.

"Georgia is my neighbor in North Carolina." Jesus, I think I'd just inserted my foot in my mouth. She was more than my neighbor. But what were we? Georgia had left that purposefully undefined.

A tight smile lit Georgia's lips. "Dinner's ready. Sit." She nodded as my dad and Sasha took a seat at the round table. I worried my bottom lip between my teeth. Georgia caught my eyes for an instant before turning and heading back into the kitchen. I followed her.

"Need any help?" I snaked an arm around her waist and pulled her hip-to-hip with me.

"No, just grabbing gravy," she murmured before

ducking out of my grip. I narrowed my eyes. Fuck, she had no reason to be like this. But I knew how women get. Two beautiful women in a room was always a potentially awkward situation.

When I wanted in the pants of one of those women and the other had embraced me in an intimate hug, it was just asking for trouble.

I sighed and followed Georgia back into the dining room. She settled herself in the chair next to my dad, which left me the chair between her and Sasha.

Complicated.

"Sasha seems nice," Georgia murmured as she readied herself for bed later that night. She pulled her jeans down her legs before slipping sleep shorts up the smooth flesh an instant later. But not so fast that I didn't catch a glimpse of the lacy black fabric of her panties. I watched from my bed, arms cocked behind my head, enjoying the view.

"Mhmm," I murmured, my eyes taking her in with a small smile on my face.

"Have you ever fucked her?"

My eyes bulged and I choked on a swallow. "What the fuck?" I narrowed my eyes at her. She'd taken me completely by surprise. Of course it would cross her mind, and Sasha had been a little touchy feely at dinner, but that's how she always was with everyone.

"You heard me." She tugged her blouse over her head and my dick twitched when she stood before me in a matching lace plunge bra. Usually, she turned around when she changed, but tonight she stood in front of me, unashamed and sexy as hell. But I could see the anger rolling off her. She was pissed. And it made her all the hotter.

"No," I answered as I stared at her tits.

"Really?" Her head shot up in surprise.

"Don't act so surprised."

"She's beautiful, and since you're a manwhore—"

"Was," I corrected her.

"*Was* a manwhore . . ." she trailed off as her cheeks pinked up with embarrassment.

"Don't be embarrassed." I crawled to the edge of the bed and wrapped her face in my hands, thumbs caressing her cheekbones. "I'm glad you asked. It was a legitimate question."

"She had her hands all over you." She pouted.

"She's a tactile person." I shrugged.

"I hated every minute," she whispered and pressed her body closer to mine.

"You know what I hate?"

"Hmm?" she hummed as she worked her lips against mine.

"Every fucking minute I have to wait before being inside you again."

She gasped before crawling up into my lap, her legs wrapped around me, her center radiating heat through the fabric of my jeans. So fucking hot.

"I can't stand not being inside you," I repeated between kisses. She moaned in response and I flipped her over on my bed, situated her beneath me, and ran my denim-covered dick between her legs.

"Nothing's stopping you," she murmured against my lips. My dick hardened further.

"Don't say that," I groaned while my hips rocked into hers of their own will.

"Why?" she breathed, her sweet breath tickling my neck.

I fisted my hands in her hair, tugging a little too hard, but I think she liked it because her body arched up into mine in the most delicious and tantalizing fucking way as a soft groan swept past her lips. I did it again and she repeated the action.

"I can't say no." I slid a bra strap down her arm and kissed the sweet flesh that was exposed.

"I don't want you to."

"Fuck, Georgia." I rocked harder into her, trying desperately to relieve the pressure of my aching cock against her hot core.

"I'm sick of waiting. Fuck me." She moaned and it was all done for me. I slid an arm around her body and released the clasp of her bra in a quick flick. She popped the button on my jeans before I lifted off her and pulled my shirt over my head with one hand. I crashed back into her and sucked in a quick breath when our bodies made hot contact again. I kissed her possessively as I pulled the bra from her arms. I dipped my head and took one puckered nipple into my mouth and sucked, laving my tongue along the peak, taking in her taste, drawing the flesh out further. She moaned and fisted her fingers in my hair, pulling and murmuring my name in my ear. It was like angels singing. The words I'd fucking dreamed about for months now.

"I finally got you in a bed," I teased, thinking back to all the other times we'd been together—on the beach, in the ocean, in the outdoor shower. I'd slept with her wrapped in my arms, but I'd never taken her in a bed.

I slid a palm down her torso. I wanted to draw this out; I wanted to fuck her as hard as I'd ever fucked anyone, but I also wanted to please her, show her pleasure she'd never felt before. I wanted to tantalize her before taking her and claiming her. My fingertips reached the end of her lace underwear and I tugged them slowly down her hips. Her hands tugged at my boxer briefs and my cock sprang from the fabric.

"Fuck please," she whimpered.

"Please what, baby?" I ordered as I kneaded her breast in my palm and sucked her nipple. Her breathing came out in sharp pants. I knew I was being rough, but I couldn't restrain myself. I'd waited so goddamn long for her.

"Make me yours." She took my dick in her hand and angled it against her soaking wet flesh. My breath ratcheted up as she slid the head of my cock between her lips, up to the hardened bud and back down again.

"You were always mine." I ground my teeth as I arched my dick up the sensitive flesh, making sure to spend extra time at her clit. The magic spot that had her draw in a sharp breath and bite her bottom lip on a moan. "This summer," I said through gritted teeth, "you were mine." I ran up her length. "When you were with him, you were mine." I teased my head at her entrance.

"Yes," she moaned and fisted her hands in her hair. I was driving her insane, turning her into a ball of hot need beneath me.

"Every fucking minute we were apart, you were mine," I groaned and slid up her length one last time before sinking into her body. Shivers overtook me as I relished our connection. I pumped in and out of her slowly, letting her adjust to me as she moaned and arched seductively. “You’ll always be mine, Georgia.”

“God, yes. Always. Always yours, Tristan. Don’t stop. Oh God, don’t stop.” she panted as I sped up and slammed into her.

“Never.” I couldn’t hold back anymore. I had to mark her, make our coupling unforgettable. Have her so strung out on me that she'd never leave me again because I couldn't survive without her. I slammed into her sweet body, our pelvic bones grinding, the sound of wet flesh and her soft moans echoing around the room. Her back arched, bringing her nipples to my lips. I sucked one into my mouth and tasted her. I twirled the elongated peak with my tongue as her body took me in. With one hand positioning me above her, one digging into the flesh of her hipbone, I dragged my teeth across her nipple as I released it and then sucked in the flesh high on her breast. Sucked and nipped, leaving an impression on her. I needed to have a piece of me on her, needed her to walk around with my mark on her body, and mostly, I needed her to see the reminder that I’d been here; that I’d been the one to give her pleasure like this, every morning that she looked in the mirror.

She groaned when I released her soft flesh from my

mouth as her nails dug into my back. She pulled and dragged her nails across my taut muscles as I pumped into her beautiful body. I sat back on my thighs and pulled her along with me, our bodies connected as I thrust up into her. Her legs straddling mine, she sat on my thighs and wrapped her arms around me, our skin connecting from hip to chest.

She moaned and arched and pulled at my hair. She was so fucking wild, so uninhibited, not the sweet girl I'd been with this summer. She was a fucking animal for me as she arched her back and took all the pleasure I was giving her and I realized then that she was staking her claim as much as I was staking mine. Having Sasha here earlier had bothered her. I'd seen the spark of jealousy in her eyes when she'd thought I wasn't looking, and that's why she'd begged me to fuck her tonight. She needed me to show her I wanted her and only her. That I was hers. I never thought a woman getting possessive over me would be so hot, but fuck if it didn't drive me more insane for her.

I glanced down at my cock pumping in and out of her sweet body. Fucking heaven. The only place I ever wanted to be. My life would be complete if I could wake up to her beautiful smile every morning and sink myself inside her beautiful body every night.

“God,” she stuttered as I felt her hot pussy clenching around my dick. I powered into her. Her moans grew erratic as she rode me. She whipped her head up and grabbed both of my shoulders. Her hair landed in a curtain around her face as she sank her teeth into my shoulder.

"Fuck, Georgia," I roared as she exploded in waves, milking my cock and making me come the hardest I could ever remembering. This fucking girl had me.

"You own me," I panted as my hips slowed their thrusting and I emptied into her. She draped her body over mine, limp like a wet rag, her breasts crushed into my chest, her body heaving and slick with sweat. I lay back on the bed as I slid out of her and held her near me. She threw an arm over her head and sighed deeply. I dipped my head into the crook of her neck and nipped at the salty flesh.

"You fucking own me," I murmured again.

"You own me, too. Completely," she breathed.

"Good. Now that this body is mine, I want it; whenever and wherever." A devilish grin turned my lips. "I'm not keeping my hands off you anymore." My inner caveman reared his alpha head. I traced a fingertip around her breast and circled in, closer to the nipple, watching it pucker. I slid the pad of my thumb across the bruise I'd left on her flesh.

"You left your mark on me." She grinned cheekily.

"Fuck, yeah, I did." I smirked up at her.

"I'd probably be pissed, but I think I left my mark too." Her eyes sparkled with amusement as she traced the spot I assumed was bruising up on my shoulder.

"Good. So it's clear to everyone we own each other. No misunderstandings," I murmured as I teased her nipple.

"Caveman."

"From manwhore to caveman—you bring it out in me, baby." I kissed her pretty pink nipple before laying my head back on the pillow and drifting off into a contented sleep.

Eight

Georgia

"Who keeps calling you?" Tristan asked, tipping his coffee cup to his lips one morning in the kitchen. Every morning since we'd left Jacksonville a week ago, we'd spent together; either at his house or mine. This morning, we were at his house. I'd come over to hang curtains and put the final touches on our little remodel that had started with the salmon paint on the walls a few weeks ago.

"Georgia?" Tristan's deep voice cut through my thoughts.

"Hmm?" I lifted my eyes from my phone.

"Who keeps calling that you're not answering?" He leaned against the counter, one palm supporting his body on the countertop, the other angled to his lips, coffee cup in hand. He looked edible. Sex on a stick personified. Just looking at him had my heart thudding. I was lost in him again.

"Don't worry about it," I murmured as I stepped closer

to him, pressing my body against his, our hips flush. I wrapped one arm around his waist and pressed my lips to his in a delicate kiss.

"Mmm, I like you pressed against me first thing in the morning," he muttered before wrapping his hand up in my hair and pulling me closer to delve into my mouth with his tongue. He devoured me. Licked me ravenously. I could feel his need growing between us. I would happily distract him like this every morning.

"Stop avoiding the question, beautiful," he murmured against my lips.

I pulled away and rolled my eyes. "You didn't seem to mind."

"Your delicious body pressed against mine? I'll never mind." He snaked one hand up my torso to squeeze my breast. "But I still want an answer."

"I don't think you'll like the answer," I said as I leaned into him, attempting to distract him again by dusting my fingertips along the waist of his low-slung jeans.

"Who is it?" He pulled away as his mossy green eyes bore into me.

I huffed in exasperation. I didn't want to tell him; in truth, I'd been trying to avoid it completely.

Tristan arched one eyebrow as he watched me.

"Kyle," I murmured and averted my eyes. The silence

echoed around his small kitchen. I shifted my legs and then chanced a glance at him. His face was hard as stone. His jaw was ticking, the only expression readable was the anger flaring in his eyes. "It's not a big deal; I haven't answered . . ." I trailed off. "Hey." I pressed my body to his and ran a hand along his jaw. I pushed up on my tiptoes and nuzzled into his neck in the place that his delicious, fresh scent was the most concentrated. "It's not a big deal." I felt his body relax against mine.

"What does he want?" he muttered.

"I have to go get my stuff. I've put it off long enough. I also have to get Diva." I hadn't known where I was going when I stormed out of the apartment I'd shared with Kyle, so I'd left some things behind until I was settled.

"Diva?"

"My cat."

"You've got a cat?"

"Yeah, you don't like cats?"

"On the contrary. I love pussies." His lips lifted in the sexiest smirk I'd ever seen.

"You've got a dirty mouth." I smacked him playfully.

"You love my dirty mouth and all the delicious things it can do to you." His lips dusted along my ear. His breath tickled my neck and shot desire straight between my legs.

"No argument there," I murmured.

"Didn't think so. Now back to this pussy," he whispered as he snaked a hand around my waist to grab my ass.

"I have to go get her. And the rest of my stuff," I rambled, distracted by his hand kneading my ass cheek.

"Right. When do we go?" He slid his arm up the back of my shirt, pulling it up my back as his fingertips slid across my flesh.

"I . . . I . . ." I couldn't think straight. "I have to go soon."

"You mean 'we.'" His lips sucked the flesh under my ear.

"No, you can't."

"Of course I can, and I will." He sucked harder, his teeth nipping, a subtle warning not to disagree.

"No, you really can't." I pushed him away a little to catch his gaze. "Kyle will flip. He knows what happened with us this summer. And he was pissed when I left. We didn't really leave on good terms and he's been threatening —"

"He's been threatening you?" His eyes hardened again. In an instant, just like that, he was back to pissed.

"No, not like that. He's just been threatening to throw everything out if I don't come get it. He even said he would take Diva to the shelter. I don't think he would, but he's pissed. I can't bring you with me."

"You don't have a choice."

"Of course I have a choice. And that's not it." I crossed my arms and glared.

"Look, this isn't coming out right." His hand wrapped around my neck and he dusted his thumb along my bottom lip. He was trying to seduce me into not being mad at him, trying to seduce me into letting him have his way.

"Stop using your sexy skills to convince me."

"Are they working?" His lips tilted on a grin. I rolled my eyes. They were so totally working. "Look, this isn't coming out right. But," he paused as his eyes searched mine for a moment, "the last time you left, it took you three months to come back." His beautiful green eyes penetrated mine the entire time.

His words swept the breath from my lungs.

"Tristan." I watched the pain register in his eyes, the memory of our time apart. "I'm coming back." I pulled his head down to mine and rested our foreheads together. He didn't respond. "Hey, do you believe that?" I pulled away and searched his eyes for his answer.

Nine

Tristan

Of course, I didn't believe it. She'd made me believe she'd be back last time too. There was no way in fuck I was letting her go without me. And then some sick realization hit—I couldn't go just to hold her hand. If she left me again, it was because she didn't want me, but fuck that, because she was mine and I was hers. It wasn't even an option anymore. Thanksgiving proved that. We belonged to each other.

The silence stretched between us in a silent standoff. I was searching for a sign that she would come back, that I could trust her. Even with Kyle.

"You said you always go back to him."

Her mouth opened and closed like a fish desperate for air. I'd shocked her.

"How can I trust you when you said you always go back

to him?" I could hear the hurt radiating in my own voice.

"Tristan." She caressed my jaw with her palm. She was trying to ease the ache and it was working; her touch was intoxicating. "I can't let you go just to babysit me."

"Why not?"

She sighed in exasperation. She was crumbling; she was going to give in. Which was good, because she really didn't have a choice in the matter.

"What would I tell him?"

"What do you mean?"

"About us? He's going to want to know."

"Fuck him. Tell him I'm your friend, your boyfriend, your lover, your neighbor; I don't give a fuck. It's not his business."

"Are you those things?" she asked.

"Well, I hope I'm your friend, and based on the proximity of our respective houses, I think I'm your neighbor—" I grinned at her, watching her shift her body and avert her eyes.

"What about the others?" she finally whispered.

"You're adorable when you're uncomfortable." My grin widened. Her eyes narrowed and she shot me a glare. "And you're irresistible when you're angry." I squeezed her ass cheek and caught her by surprise.

"You're impossible."

"And you love it." I slid my hand down the curve of her ass and snaked my fingers between her legs.

"Irritating too," she said just before her eyes fluttered back on a moan.

"I hope I'm all of those things, Georgia," I said seriously, as I searched her beautiful face. Her neck arched as I caressed the damp flesh between her legs.

"What?" she whimpered.

"Your friend, your boyfriend, your lover, your neighbor. I hope I'm all of those things."

"Oh." Her breath whooshed out. "My boyfriend?"

"If you'll have me." I grinned and caught her lips in a kiss. I was using my charm to convince her. I knew it and I did it without shame. I was playing the cards I'd been dealt, and I played them well. She fisted her hands in my hair and arched her body into mine. I caught her with an arm behind her back as she bowed and I took her lips, ravishing her. I kissed her like my life depended on it, because it did. My life depended on her being in it. On her answer. I couldn't give her the option of saying no.

"I'm afraid," she murmured as she pulled back to take a breath.

"Of?" I bent over her and captured her lips with mine again, snaking my hand down her thigh and hitching it over my hips.

"Us."

"Why?" She was being candid, and I needed to take advantage. She held things inside so much. I needed her to talk. I needed to know what I was working with.

"Your history. Our history," she breathed.

"What do you mean?" I pulled my lips away from hers and searched out her beautiful browns. Her eyes were hooded with lust and her eyelashes were so long they shaded her high cheekbones. She was completely fucking breathtaking.

"I'm afraid . . . your history and what Kyle did to me . . . I'm just afraid."

"Stop speaking in code, babe. What did Kyle do to you?"

Her chest continued to heave beneath me. She was still so turned on, it took every ounce of my energy not to forgo the conversation and take her right there on my floor. But I needed the answer. I needed to know what the obstacles were, if any.

"He cheated on me," she murmured. Lust overrode any pain that she might have felt at saying those words.

"When?"

"For years, off and on. And with your history, I don't know if I can trust—"

"Don't do that. I'm not him. My history means shit. I

would never, ever fucking cheat on you. You're all I need. Do you hear me?" I tipped her chin up to meet my eyes. Her browns widened as she took me in. "I have never cheated on anyone and I'm not starting now. I told you—you're it for me, end of story. Don't put Kyle's shit on me. He's an idiot who didn't know what he had. I can tell you, Georgia, I will never make that mistake with you. I know exactly what I have and she's loving, and empathetic, and beautiful and sexy and irresistible. And mine." She stared at me as I finished. I waited breathlessly for her reaction. Finally, she took my head in her hands and pulled me to her in a ravenous kiss. I held her fiercely to my body as she crawled up me and locked her legs around my waist.

"I take it that's a yes?" I murmured between kisses.

"Smart ass." She nipped me playfully.

"You've got a dirty mouth too, beautiful." I grinned at her. "Makes me hot as fuck."

"Oh my God." She laughed and pulled away from me.

"So no more taking it slow?"

She peered up at me through her eyelashes and shook her head, a soft smile spreading across her face. It took my fucking breath away.

"And your boyfriend is going with you to collect your things, including your pussy?" I arched a playful eyebrow at her. She narrowed her eyes at me as she tried to hide the smile tugging at her lips.

"That's what I thought. Now make me breakfast, woman."

"I don't think so, dear." She planted her hands on her hips after I'd released her from my iron grip. It was so fucking hot.

"I've got a conference call, and your man is starving." I lifted my shirt and rubbed my stomach with a frown. Her eyes flickered down to land on my abs and I watched them darken with lust. So the girl had a thing for my abs? I'd have to remember to use that to my advantage next time around.

"What do you want?" she asked without tearing her eyes from my stomach. I laughed a full-bellied laugh and pulled her into my arms, kissing her forehead.

"Toast and orange juice is fine." I couldn't tear the grin from my face.

Owned me.

This girl completely fucking owned me and I loved every minute.

Ten

Tristan

"You ready for this?" I squeezed her knee as she directed me to Kyle's apartment building in DC.

"As I'll ever be," she huffed and then opened the door of the Jeep.

"Hey." I slipped a palm around her neck and brought her against me. I rested my forehead against hers as we huddled over the console. "Everything's going to be okay," I murmured before brushing my lips against hers.

"Yep." She nodded, but I could tell she was still worried. I frowned and massaged her neck before letting her go. We stepped out into the cold December air. She'd finally agreed to let me come up to DC with her to collect her things and now here we were, the weekend before Christmas, and I was about to see her douchebag ex for the first time since the summer.

Georgia finally confessed he'd been harassing her with

phone calls and texts, threatening to come down, begging her to talk to him, insisting he would throw her stuff away or bring it to the beach house for her. Neither was a viable option. I didn't want him anywhere near her in North Carolina, especially if he was as unstable as he sounded.

We walked up the steps and took the elevator to his floor. She slowed as we approached the apartment door, hesitation and dread pouring off her body. I grabbed her hand in mine and brought her knuckles to my lips for a kiss.

“It’s going to be okay.”

She nodded and then dropped my hand from hers. She tapped softly at the door.

“Georgia, God, it’s so good to see you.” Kyle swung the door open and looked about to embrace Georgia before his eyes landed on me. Confusion and then anger flared. His jaw hardened. “What’s he doing here?” he asked, without tearing his gaze from mine. I clenched my fists at my sides. So he wasn’t going to make this easy.

“He’s here to help.”

“I could have helped. We didn’t need him, Georgia.” Kyle tore his eyes from mine and back to her. He stretched his arms and scooped her against his body in a hug that was more than friendly and lasted way too fucking long in my opinion. I narrowed my eyes and waited for her to push him away. She recoiled as he slid his hands up her back and then his gaze caught mine again. The asshole was doing this for my benefit. I clenched my teeth, waiting for her to take action because if she didn't, I was going to fucking annihilate this guy and not think twice about it.

Finally, Georgia pushed him away with a weak smile. He moved aside and we strode into the apartment. A white puffball of a cat sauntered up and curled itself around Georgia's legs.

"Hey, sweetheart, I've missed you." My beautiful girlfriend nuzzled into the cat's fur while Kyle watched her and I watched him. Georgia showered attention on her pussy for a few minutes, which made me a sick fuck because I kind of liked the sound of that, before glancing around the apartment.

"I thought you had my stuff in boxes?" She tilted her head and looked at Kyle.

"A few things, I didn't have time—"

"You said you were throwing out everything if I wasn't here to get it this weekend." Her gaze cut to him and I was sure she was shooting daggers. She was pissed and I was ready for her to lay into him. I also wondered if Kyle got turned on as much as I did when she was all angry and hot. And then I was pissed again and wanted to kidnap her and her pussy and leave everything else behind, mostly Kyle.

"I wouldn't have. I just wanted to see you. We need to

talk, which is why I'm kinda fucking pissed that you brought this guy. He your bodyguard? Come on, Georgia. We were together for years, and you just left. I wanted to talk and you never answered my calls. You owe me a conversation."

"She owes you nothing," I spat.

His eyebrow arched at me. "Not your concern, buddy. Just talk to me for a minute, in private." He glanced from her to me.

"Not happening." I stepped closer to her.

"Okay, stop with the pissing contest. I'll talk to you for a minute, Kyle, but that's it. I'm here to get my stuff and I'm leaving."

"Sure, babe." Kyle placed a hand at her back and guided her down a hallway, a sneer on his face as he glanced back at me. What was she thinking? I was here so she wouldn't have to be alone with him. I was her fucking boyfriend and here she was ducking off into a room to have private time with her ex? Not fucking cool. My blood was boiling.

And then I remembered all the things she'd said to me about her past and Kyle's place in it. Like it or not, he'd played a big part of who she was, so I needed to let her talk to him if she felt she needed to for the sake of closure and all that. Only my stomach was rolling at the thought of him convincing her to stay.

I looked around the apartment they'd shared and found it hollow. Perfect—like out of a magazine. So perfect, as if no one lived there. Her beach house was so much more *her;* it looked like whoever lived here was void of personality. I couldn't even pick out what might be Georgia's. I took a few steps farther into the living room and my eyes landed on the mantle with framed pictures: her and Kyle together, Drew and Silas in college, the four of them, a young couple with a baby in their arms. I squinted and held the last picture up; it looked like the baby could be Georgia, presumably with her parents. She was a sweet baby with the roundest cheeks I'd ever seen. Chubby legs and a shock of dark hair. Her mom's bright smile mirrored her own. She was the spitting image of her mother, except for her eyes. Her dad had shocking dark eyes and heavily lined eyelashes. He sat on a bench, his wife at his side, a protective arm wrapped around her shoulder and a squirming baby Georgia in her arms. So unaware of the pain that would hit them nearly a decade later. A night when Georgia's parents would be ripped from her life.

"I'm not doing this with you, Kyle." Georgia stomped out of the room, cat still in her arms. "Hang onto her." She thrust the cat in my hands. Diva looked up at me, eyes narrowed. I was sure the cat was glaring at me. Maybe she smelled Charlie and wasn't impressed.

Georgia stomped back to the room she'd just exited and I heard a bang and heated whispers before I walked after her. I knew Kyle was fucking with her head, trying to cajole her, guilt-trip her, do anything he could to get her to stay, but my girl was going home with me.

"Don't fucking touch me," I heard her bite out. I dashed into the bedroom and found her shoving him away from her body, a suitcase and a duffle bag at her feet. My eyes flared and my jaw clenched when he tried to go back to her, his eyes pleading.

"Baby, come on; this is you and me. Don't let whatever you think you have with him get in the way of us. I know his type; he won't be around for long, Georgia. It's always been us."

"You need to shut the fuck up." I glared as I stepped closer to them, Diva still in one arm, my other fist clenched.

"Back the fuck off; you don't even know her. Who do you think has had her from the beginning? She's not leaving me, man. Georgia won't leave me. She's too fucking scared of the unknown to leave," he sneered at me. I pulled my arm back, cat in one hand, arm cocked in the other, ready to land a blow to his smug face, when Georgia's fist shot into my line of vision and landed on Kyle's cheekbone. He spun and looked at her, eyes wide with shock.

"What the fuck, Georgia?" he roared as his other hand grabbed at her neck.

Oh, fuck no.

"Get your fucking hands off her." I barreled, shoving him away before landing a fist square on his nose. He spun and landed on the floor, his hand cupping his face and blood pooling in his fingers. With Diva still perched in my arms, a front row seat to the destruction, I leaned over Kyle and landed two more blows to his jaw and his cheekbone in quick succession.

"Fuck, get off me. Are you crazy?" Kyle screamed as blood splattered.

"You touched her. Don't do it again. Ever. Don't fucking touch her. Don't fucking call her. And don't think you'll ever fucking see her again." I landed one more blow and his eye started swelling immediately.

"Get some shit, Georgia. I'll hire someone to come back and get anything else." I pulled her out of the room by the arm. She yanked out of my grip, ran to Kyle, and landed one swift kick in his gut.

"Fuck!" He hunched over painfully.

"Asshole," she sneered. That was my girl. So fucking hot when she was pissed. She grabbed a bag and threw personal items into it. She sprinted into the living room and pulled picture frames off the mantel, leaving the ones of her and Kyle.

"I'm done; let's go." She finally looked at me.

"Just remember." Kyle leaned against the doorframe, hand still cupping his nose, blood dripping down his shirt. "I had her first and I'll have her last. Don't forget that." His eyes cut from me to her, a sickening sneer on his face. His words felt like a threat as much as a statement.

"Fuck off," Georgia shot at him before she grabbed my hand and we walked out the door, leaving it swinging on the hinges.

"Jesus, are you okay?" Georgia wet a napkin with water and swiped blood off my face while Diva meowed obnoxiously from the backseat. We were stopped at a Starbucks parking lot a few blocks from her old apartment.

"I'm great." I grinned and caught her wrist in my hand and pulled her lips to mine. "So fucking hot," I whispered.

"What?" She pulled away, her eyebrows knit together in confusion.

"You know how hot it makes me when you're angry, babe. You kicked his ass. You threw the first punch. I'm hard as a fucking rock right now."

"Tristan." She giggled before I pulled her to me again. I

pressed her lips to mine, pulling her into my lap, desperate to take her right here, regardless of who could see.

"Move in with me," I breathed between kisses.

"What?" Her chest heaved with pants. I'd stolen her breath from kissing her. I wanted to steal her heart too. I hadn't thought about asking her to move in with me before the words came out of my mouth. But there they were and I didn't regret them.

"Move in with me." I nipped at her lips again as my hands went up her shirt to knead her breasts.

"You're crazy." She pushed my hands out of her shirt.

"Crazy for you," I flirted.

"And corny." She rolled her eyes.

"Move in with me. My place is smaller, easier to maintain, plus you're renting the beach house out in the spring, right? Let's get you moved in now, then you can list the house." This idea was sounding better and fucking better the more I attempted to convince her.

Her eyes searched my face, I was assuming to look for any ounce of hesitation on my part. She wouldn't find it.

"You wanna live with me?" she murmured, her eyes all hooded and sexy again.

I held her tightly to me, caressing her back with an open palm. "Absolutely."

"But I snore."

"Not any louder than I do."

"And I steal the covers," she whispered.

"Don't need any. Having your hot body wrapped around mine is heat enough."

"So fucking corny." She rolled her eyes again and I tilted my head and took her lips with mine.

I kissed her and ran my hands up her back, grinding my hips into hers as she fisted her hands in my hair and arched her body against mine. "Say yes," I murmured.

"Yes," she breathed and I took her lips again because she was one step closer to being mine forever.

Eleven

Tristan

"So then she hauls back and lands a kick right to his gut," I gushed as Gavin and I sat in the living room, drinking beer. The Disney Christmas Day Parade played on the TV screen in front of us—something Georgia insisted on watching. While I teased her about it relentlessly, secretly I thought it was utterly adorable.

"Fuck, that's hot."

"Really fucking hot." I agreed with him. He knew all about the power of anger when it came to sex. All that passion and rage bottled up? Really fucking hot.

"You kicked him, Georgia?" Drew squealed from the kitchen. Georgia only shrugged, but the grin spread wide across her face told me she was proud of herself.

"I always knew you were a superwoman," Silas, Georgia's gay best friend, chimed in from the dining room. He and his boyfriend Justin were setting the table for Christmas dinner. The house smelled delicious, like ham and mashed potatoes and pies. Heaven. Especially because Georgia was there, my girl, cooking us a feast. I'd helped however I could: opening the wine, making the mashed potatoes, goosing her when she'd bent to take the ham out of the oven.

"Charlie, out of the kitchen." I pointed and the old dog gave me a sidelong glance, trotting back to the living room. Diva curled around Georgia's feet, a loud meow releasing from her throat. She was begging for scraps just as much as Charlie'd been, but her name was Diva for a reason; that cat got away with everything. When we'd brought her home last week Charlie had stuck his big nose in her face, she'd given him one fierce swat, and their relationship had been established—Diva ruled the roost.

"Time to eat," Georgia sang from the kitchen as she carried the ham to the table. "Come slice, babe." She looked at me and I was drawn to her like a moth to a flame. I set my beer on the counter and went to her without another thought. I wrapped an arm around her waist, so fucking thankful to share Christmas together—with her and our friends. I landed a kiss on the top of her head and she returned the sentiment with a peck on my lips.

"You look beautiful," I muttered into her hair.

"Thanks." She tucked her head under my chin with a smile.

"Cut the sloppy shit; I'm starving." Gavin plopped on a chair. I chuckled and then took the electric knife in hand and prepared to slice the ham.

"We've got an announcement." Drew leaned into Gavin's chest, her hand splayed across his leg after we'd finished eating, our bellies stretched to the max, with half empty wine glasses in front of us.

"So do we." Georgia chanced a glance at me and I gave her neck a soft squeeze.

"Us first."

"Okay." Georgia laughed.

"We're pregnant."

"What?" Georgia choked on her wine.

"Seriously?" I shot a glance to Gavin. The wide grin on his face confirmed what Drew had said. Also that he was happy about it. Really fucking happy. "Congrats, man." I grinned.

"Drew, aren't you on birth control?" This clearly hadn't yet sunk in for Georgia.

"I was. I was so busy catching up on work after summer, I forgot to refill my prescription." Drew shrugged.

"Wait, after summer? How far along are you?"

"Thirteen weeks. We're due May 28." The grin split across her face.

"In spring? Jesus, Drew. How come you didn't tell me?"

"I didn't find out until I was almost ten weeks along. I was so caught up in everything, I sorta forgot that I hadn't had my period."

"God, TMI," Silas whined from across the table.

"Wow. Congratulations," Georgia murmured.

"I can't believe you're going to be a parent. What kind of world is this?" Silas teased. "Congrats, Daddy. Hopefully, he or she takes after you." He winked at Gavin.

"Be nice." Justin shouldered Silas.

"Yeah, be nice to me while I'm with child."

"Oh my God, and so it starts," Silas muttered.

"When do we find out if it's a boy or girl?" The excitement in Georgia's voice grew.

"We have an early ultrasound scheduled in a few weeks. I hope it's a girl. Imagine all the little dresses and headbands."

"A girl, man?" I cocked an eyebrow at Gavin. "You're in trouble if you have a girl."

"A mini-Drew? Christ, can you imagine?" Silas jibed.

"Hey." Drew glared at him.

"I don't care what it is, as long as it's healthy." Gavin

leaned into Drew and rubbed her tummy. It was the sweetest thing I'd ever seen. I glanced over at Georgia and watched her watching them. Her features had softened as a thoughtful look crossed her face.

"Wait, you have an announcement too, right?" Drew perked up and glanced at Georgia. "Oh my God. Are you pregnant too? That would be amazing! Our kids could grow up together."

My eyes widened in surprise.

Georgia? *Pregnant?*

"No, I'm not pregnant," she said as she looked over at me, a sheepish look on her face. "We're moving in together," she finished.

"That's great." Drew beamed.

"Really?" Silas frowned.

"Yeah, after the new year, we're going to start moving my stuff in. I need to rent the beach house next summer, so it just made the most sense."

"You make it sound like a business arrangement." Drew frowned.

"No, it's just convenient."

My jaw ticked at her words. I was convenient?

Irritation flared in my stomach. I didn't like the sound of that at all.

Twelve

Georgia

"A convenient business arrangement? Is that what I am to you?" He had me pinned underneath him in bed later that night.

"I didn't mean it like that," I breathed as he skimmed his hand up my torso and pulled the shirt over my head.

"How was it meant?" he muttered as he pulled at the cup of my bra with his teeth. My tummy fluttered and rolled, anxious to feel skin on skin. Holidays were tough for me, always tough. It was so easy for me to get lost in my head with the memories, but Tristan was what I needed to keep me in the present. And he did an epic job of it.

"I just meant . . ." I groaned as he pulled down the cup of my bra, bringing my puckering flesh to his mouth. His lips wrapped around my nipple and lightning bolts of desire flamed cross my body and landed in a pool between my legs. I shifted underneath him on a moan.

"You just meant what?" He pulled away and blew warm breath across my hardened peak.

"Oh God." I threaded my fingers in his long hair and pulled his lips back to my chest.

"That's what I thought." He nuzzled my breast before latching onto my nipple again. "Last I checked, business arrangements didn't include my head between your legs." Goose bumps erupted across my skin as he breathed his way down my stomach. "Are we a business arrangement, Georgia?" He hooked his fingertips under the lace of my panties at my hips.

"God, no," I breathed.

"Am I just convenient for you?" he murmured as he peeled my panties off my legs and nuzzled my wet and throbbing center with his nose.

"Never," I choked.

"Is this something you would do with a business partner?" He dragged his tongue up my length and nipped at my clit when he reached the top.

"Never." I tightened my legs around his head, desperate for him not to move.

"This is for me, your *boyfriend*. The boyfriend that you live with." He thrust two fingers into my heat and I bucked underneath him. His lips latched around my clit and he sucked so hard, stars burst behind my closed eyelids. My hands fisted in his hair and pulled him tighter to me. I moaned and panted his name as he worked his fingers in and out. He laved his tongue up my wet heat, back and forth, teasing the swollen flesh before he added a third finger. I bucked and writhed and, with two long draws, an orgasm ripped through me, the likes of which I'd never felt before. My legs shook and tightened around his head as he continued to suck and nurse the orgasm from my body. His fingers slowed their thrusting before he finally eased them out of me.

I lay against the white sheets of his king-sized bed, limp and sated.

Breathing heavily, a smile dancing across my lips, I murmured, "I knew there was a reason why I kept you around."

One eyebrow ticked up as he crawled up my body. The hand still between my breasts darted over to give my nipple a rough pinch. "Watch it, baby."

My eyes fluttered open and I took in his beautiful face. A few locks of hair fell across his forehead and he looked utterly delicious. I reached a hand up to cup his cheek, my thumb running across his full bottom lip, still glistening from my juices.

"You've got a talent the likes of which I've never seen before." A smile split across my face as I teased him.

"Worth the risk?" His eyes sparkled in that mesmerizing way.

"Worth every risk," I murmured before pulling his head down to me and plastering a long, drawn out kiss on his lips. Our tongues mingled and explored. He slipped a hand in my tangled locks and massaged my scalp.

"You're worth everything to me," he murmured as he slid his jeans and boxers down his legs and kicked them off. "I'd do it all for you. Do it all over again. Go back to the very start. You're worth every risk." He eased into me and slowly worked in and out. Each push in and each draw out dragged across every sensitized nerve ending I had, and so many more I hadn't even known existed. I shuddered as he eased out to the tip, and the air escaped my lungs in a pleasurable rush when he eased back in, taking it slow, savoring every inch. My eyelids fluttered closed as I enjoyed his skin pressed to mine.

"Eyes, Georgia. I want to see your eyes when I'm inside you."

My eyes shot open and found his lovely deep green orbs burning into me, taking my breath away, just like they always did.

"This," he motioned between us. "We aren't convenient. We're everything." He emphasized each word with one delicious pull out, one delicious push back in. My nerves fired off, little fireworks shooting across my body. I laced my legs around his waist and held him tight to me so he couldn't ease all the way out again. I couldn't lose him, not for another instant.

"We're everything," I repeated and locked my arms around his neck, holding onto him with every muscle I had. "You're everything," I murmured in his ear. He sucked in a sharp breath as if I'd caught him by surprise.

Thirteen

Tristan

Fuck, she'd taken my breath away.

Every minute, she took my breath away.

Every smile, every movement, every word—an endless array of stolen breaths.

She hadn't said those words, those three words we'd each said once this summer, and I wondered if she still felt them. They threatened to burst through at every emotionally charged moment, and it was becoming harder and harder for me to keep them in. I felt everything with this girl, and it was becoming nearly unbearable for me not to share it with her. I knew I had to let her take the lead, though. I was terrified of running her off, scaring her back to him. I knew what she'd told me—he was what she knew, and she always went back—one wrong step and she could jump in her car and drive right back to him and that would be it for us.

Pain twisted my stomach at the thought of seeing her drive away again. I couldn't bear it. I just wasn't sure if she was feeling it too and if she was ready to take this step with me. I'd already stuck my fucking foot in my mouth when I'd asked her to move in with me. Thankfully, it had worked out and I hadn't scared her off, but I'd seen the indecision in her eyes.

I always wondered if, when things got too real, she thought of him.

I also wondered how much he was contacting her. The phone calls didn't seem to be so often now that we'd picked up her stuff, but once in a while, I still saw her look down with a frown marring her stunning features. I was trying my best not to lose her trust, but every fucking time I saw her phone sitting somewhere, I wanted to snatch it and go through her calls, check her texts to see what he was saying.

I breathed deeper, emotion choking my throat and causing my heart to beat overtime. I thrust in and out; her tight body took me in. Letting me fill her was so overwhelming that I thought I might lose my mind. She'd done me in with her words.

I was her everything.

And she was mine.

I captured her lips in a rough kiss as I tried to tell her without words just how much she owned me. Her walls started to quiver around me and I lost it. She clawed my back as another orgasm tore through her body. I pumped and growled into her mouth, my lips refusing to detach from hers as I released everything I had into her. Suddenly, Gavin and Drew's announcement crossed my brain and I wanted to plant my seed in Georgia. I wanted to have a piece of me inside of her, something that connected us forever. Something that we could share.

I swallowed the lump that had lodged in my throat at the thought of Georgia, hugely pregnant with my baby, walking barefoot on the beach. She took my fucking breath away, just like she always did.

"Fuck," I moaned. I wanted to tell her I loved her, but forced myself to wait.

Fourteen

Georgia

The cold air bit at my cheeks as I hustled from my car to Tristan's house—our house. It was still hard for me to get used to the fact that we were living together. The moving truck had come this morning and delivered the rest of my items from Kyle's apartment—mainly my beloved antique bedroom set that had been my parents.

I'd just come in from running errands and tossed my bag on the counter before searching out my sexy boyfriend. I found him in his office, laptop open, legs spread wide as he relaxed in his chair. He was talking to Gavin on speakerphone when I plopped myself in his lap and curled around his body. I shivered from the leftover chill from the February air.

I smacked a kiss on his lips as he rubbed his open palm up and down my back, while he and Gavin talked about an account that needed special attention. Something about security and encryption and more gibberish that flew straight over my head. Tristan snaked his fingertips under my sweater and dug his fingers into my hip, tickling me in a spot where he knew I was helpless. I whipped around on a giggle and grabbed his wrist. His sculpted lips turned down in a sexy pout.

"Hey, Georgia," Gavin greeted me over the line.

"Hey, Gav. How's Drew?"

"Bitching and moaning about pregnancy, but beautiful as ever."

"Aww."

Tristan rolled his eyes. "Such a fucking sap."

"Hey, man, you just wait. Most beautiful fucking thing ever to see Drew carrying my kid. Takes my breath away every time I see her." I heard Drew "aw" in the background before small kissing noises filtered through the phone speaker.

"Jesus," Tristan groaned.

"Hey, Tristan," Drew chirped. "Georgia, call me later, okay?"

"Yep." I grinned as I pecked Tristan on the lips.

"Hey, man. Back to the account, before we were so rudely interrupted." Tristan goosed me on the ass. I winked at him before slipping the mail off his desk and rifling through it as I made my way out the door. I sped through the electric and heating bills, something from the marina to do with Tristan's boat, and then my eyes landed on *Washington DC Department of Corrections*. My heart thudded in my ears and my breath caught painfully in my throat. I hadn't seen an envelope with this return address in years.

Exactly sixteen years.

My mind went blank as I warred with myself about opening it. I wanted to throw it away, burn it, and never see it again.

I dropped the rest of the mail on the floor and tore the envelope open, letting the ripped paper flutter to the floor. I unfolded the letter and read the first line before skimming the rest of the paragraph. I licked my lips as the letter danced to the floor, landing at my feet.

I turned and my eyes caught Tristan's. His beautiful green irises stared back at me, concern etched across his face. I licked my lips nervously. I felt like my body would crumble.

I couldn't hold myself up.

I was falling.

Free falling back where I'd been sixteen years ago.

Pain cracked open my chest and my heart thudded hard and fast, so fast I thought I might have a heart attack. I blinked back tears and tried to take deep breaths. Tristan said something before hanging up the phone and shooting out of his chair toward me. I couldn't hear a fucking thing. My heart roared in my ears. The roar of the waves outside the house was deafening.

Parole.

Eligible for parole.

A hearing.

Your presence for a statement.

My legs gave out just as Tristan reached me, his arms wrapping around my waist as we crumpled in a mess of limbs on the floor. I laid my head across his shoulder and inhaled his soothing, fresh scent. The now familiar smell of him brought tears to my eyes. I was thankful that he was here and with me. Thankful I had someone to soothe me.

He rubbed calming caresses across my back and begged me to tell him what was wrong. Finally, he gave up and his eyes darted to the letter I'd torn open on the floor. He snagged it and perused the sentences quickly.

"Jesus Christ," he muttered as he began sliding his palms all over my back, soothing me, shushing in my ear, rubbing my neck with deft fingers.

It was all coming back. A rewind of sixteen years. Except now, I had Tristan. Kyle was absent and in his place was Tristan.

I felt my stomach roll with sickness. I lurched from the floor and lunged for the toilet in the bathroom. I emptied the contents of my stomach and spent equal time sobbing and hyperventilating. My past was replaying just when I'd thought I'd finally embraced my future.

"You don't have to do it, you know." Tristan lifted me into his lap from my place on the couch.

"I don't want to talk about it," I mumbled, eyes trained on the television in front of us, not seeing the show flashing on the screen. Another crime drama that Tristan was obsessed with. I looked, yet didn't watch at all.

I'd been telling him all night that I didn't want to talk about it. He'd stayed silent, we'd stayed silent, and on the rare occasion he'd mentioned it, even in passing, I'd had the same answer.

I don't want to talk about it.

"Okay," he soothed as his hand ran circles up and down my back. Diva jumped up on my leg and nudged her head against my hand.

"Hey, honey," I murmured and stroked her soft fur. She purred and began digging her nails into Tristan's thigh in appreciation.

"Ow." His brow furrowed in the most adorable way. He tried to nudge her away, but she wouldn't hear it. She'd found a new best friend in Tristan. He spent most of his time with Charlie—he was a dog person through and through—but he never turned down my high maintenance baby girl when she came calling after his affections.

"Be nice." I lifted her into my arms and nuzzled my nose into the soft fur at her neck. I inhaled and stroked her as she purred. I closed my eyes and tried to stay in the moment. Tried to stop thinking about going back to DC and standing before the parole board, reliving my experience one terrible night sixteen years ago when my parents were murdered, because that was what it would be like. If there was ever anything I needed to put in my past, it was this. It was so easy for me to fall back into it again. I needed to guard my heart before the emotion and pain took over.

In the present, I was sitting on the lap of my gorgeous, open-hearted boyfriend, who wanted nothing more than the best for me. I sat Diva on the couch next to us and turned to him.

"Thanks," I whispered as I tucked my head into his neck. I inhaled his intoxicating scent and sighed. My lips worked across the soft skin in the hollow where his neck met his shoulder.

"For what?" he asked. His voice had dropped an octave, his palms on my back rubbing a little rougher, his heart thudding a little quicker.

"For being here, with me." I wrapped my arms around his neck and tangled my fingers into the hair at his nape.

"Only place I want to be." He pushed his hands into my hair and pulled my head away to gaze into my eyes. "You know that, right?" He dipped his head to lock me with his searing green eyes.

"Yes," I whispered and angled into his lips, taking his mouth with mine in a slow kiss. I explored his lips, savored the taste of him, the feel of his soft flesh against my own. I caressed his cheekbone with my thumb and committed his beautiful face to muscle memory. I feared that there was a tough road ahead for me and I wanted to call on these moments with him to get me through.

"I . . . Tristan, I . . ." I murmured against his lips, unable to finish my thought.

"Go on." He quirked one beautiful eyebrow at me with a lopsided grin. He knew what I was thinking and he was teasing me. The bastard was teasing me just when I was feeling the most vulnerable.

"You're a shit." I pushed against his shoulder.

"I'm your shit." His grin widened for a moment before he pulled me back to him and captured my lips with his. His kiss was rougher, needier, and I loved it.

"I love us." I pulled away and locked his eyes with mine. "I just want you to know I really love what we have."

I worked my thumbs along the contours of his face. It was the best I could give him at the moment.

He stared back at me for a few breathless moments. He looked like he was warring with something. "I know," he finally said.

"Good." I pressed a kiss to his lips. The lips I relished in, savored and devoured in equal parts. He kissed me back, exploring my mouth with his tongue, his hands running up the inside of my sweater to settle just beneath my breasts. I couldn't get enough of him. I wanted to eat him. Discover every inch of his body with my tongue. Starting with those pouty, sculpted lips that I couldn't get enough of.

I moaned and arched into him just before my phone rang out.

"Shit, I bet that's Drew." I pulled away from his lips.

"Let it go." He tried to reattach his lips to mine.

"She'll keep calling. There's no escaping her." I lifted off his lap.

A tortured groan escaped his throat. He flung his head back on the couch, his eyes squeezed shut. He looked utterly adorable.

"Save it for later because I want these—" I traced my thumb along the outline of his lips. "—all over my body tonight."

"Christ." Another groan as he scrubbed his hands over

his face and into his too long hair. "You love to torture me."

"It isn't hard to do." I winked at him as I walked to grab my phone.

"Vixen," Tristan growled before not so obliviously readjusting the tent in his jeans.

Fifteen

Tristan

She was a fucking vixen and she knew it. She loved torturing me, and I loved it. The only thing I loved more than her torturing me about being inside her was actually being inside her.

I was a masochist, without a doubt. At least when it came to Georgia.

I heaved a sigh and stood to try and walk off the excess energy. Charlie jumped up and gave his tail a wag.

"Outside, boy?" I gave him a scratch before opening the French doors to let him out. He ambled down the steps and turned the corner of the house. I walked back to the TV and turned it off, meaning to step outside to keep an eye on Charlie, until I heard Georgia's voice.

She sounded sad and forlorn and I instantly knew why.

She was talking to Drew about the letter. Telling her what it meant. Her fears about reliving the past and that night when two strangers had broken into her house and robbed and murdered her parents, all while a twelve-year-old Georgia hid under her bed.

I clenched my jaw when I heard Kyle's name. Why the fuck had Kyle been brought up?

Dammit, I loved living on the beach just as much as the next guy, but the constant roar of the waves made eavesdropping pretty fucking difficult. I found myself taking a step down the hallway with the intention of hearing better before I caught myself.

I couldn't listen to this. This was a private conversation, and it hurt like hell that she was opening up to Drew and not to me, but I understood it. She'd hunkered off to our bedroom for a reason; she'd wanted privacy.

I ran a hand through my hair and gave a rough yank before turning around and heading out the door to keep an eye on Charlie.

I ran my hands along the wood grain of the deck railing and let my thoughts run wild. I didn't know if Georgia would go back and make an appearance for the hearing, but if she did, she would be back in DC, and back with Kyle; the one person she'd always relied on to get her through this shit when it came up.

It'd been sixteen years, would she still fall into old habits? I had no doubt that Kyle would try and convince her to stay with him and use every manipulative tool at his disposal. While I certainly wanted to fight for her—she was worth it to me, she was worth everything—it was against my grain to fight for someone. If she didn't want to be with me, I wasn't going to lower myself so far as to beg her to stay. If Georgia was going to fall back into her old life, then so be it.

That thought terrified me more than anything else, but I knew it would be hard for her to stay. Every fucking day, I saw it on her face. The battle she waged between her old life and our new one. I held my breath every time her phone rang. Gritted my teeth when I saw Kyle's name flash across the screen. Deep fucking down in my pain-ravaged heart, I was afraid this time would be the time he finally convinced her to go back, because deep fucking down I didn't have faith she would stay.

I didn't have faith she would break the mold for me, and I knew I wasn't fucking worth it—knew my past was colored with poor decisions. That was a real kick to the gut; I didn't deserve her. I'd done so much I now regretted, I couldn't be surprised when she finally came to her senses and walked away.

I ran another angry hand through my hair and called for Charlie. I needed a beer and to plop myself in front of some mindless TV show to get this endless cycle of negative thinking off my mind. Or maybe do some work. Gavin and I had a big account that needed some attention. The CEO was a bastard who wanted his hand held through the entire process.

Charlie trotted up the stairs and we headed back into the kitchen. I tossed him a treat and then padded down to the spare room I used as an office. I closed the door behind me and settled into my desk chair for a long night of throwing myself into the comfortable mundane-ness of codes and numbers.

Sixteen

Georgia

"Hey, love." I heard Silas's voice loud and clear over the phone.

"Wrong person." Tristan grinned. "But it's great to hear your voice too." A sexy smile tipped his mouth. I wanted him to hang up on my best friend immediately so I could attack those lips. It had been a few days and I still hadn't spoken to Tristan much about the letter but my mind had been consumed by it. The nightmares had returned; the previous two nights I'd woken up in a cold sweat, memories of that night playing on repeat in my mind. It was the first time I'd had a nightmare since coming back to the beach and now here I was, thrown back into the darkness.

I tried to keep my mind off the parole hearing during the day by marketing the rental. I'd posted it on some websites and had a local realtor who specialized in summer rentals walk through. I had inheritance and life insurance money in the bank account, but I'd been taking so much from it over the last year that I needed to start renting this house and get some funds going back in.

"Here she is." Tristan handed the phone to me. I placed a peck on his cheek and then put the phone to my ear.

"How's it going, baby girl?" I heard the grin in Silas's voice from across the phone line. I pictured his brown eyes dancing, his blond hair styled just perfectly. My mood instantly lifted.

"It's okay."

"That doesn't sound like okay."

I sighed and picked at the frayed edges of a hole in my jeans.

"Spill, love." Silas hit me with the sternest voice he could muster. It worked like a charm.

"I got a letter." I turned to frown at Tristan. I really didn't want to get into this at all. He rubbed my leg. I'd only just gotten it a few days ago, spilled my guts to Drew last night, still hadn't spoken much to Tristan about it, and yet here I was. I heaved a sigh and lifted off the couch, headed for the kitchen and a bottle of wine.

Tristan followed me in and took the bottle from my hands, mouthing that he'd take care of it. I smiled at him thankfully before I started in on the letter I'd received and how I was feeling. Tristan tried not to hover, although he rubbed my neck every now and again when I was especially tense. That was until the wine seeped through my veins and had tingles lighting up my body.

I relaxed as I finished my story, telling him I needed to go back to DC for the hearing in May, a few months from now. My best friend listened patiently, murmuring and offering comfort when necessary.

"I wish you were here," I finished dejectedly.

"Me too, love," Silas answered.

"So enough of this sad stuff. Can we talk about you? How's Justin?" I took a long draw of my wine.

"Well, we're moving down there."

"What?" I squeaked.

"I'm letting the lease go on my place. Moving in with Justin in the spring."

'Oh God, Silas! I'm so excited."

"We can't be apart, love. Not good for either one of us." Silas laughed.

"Definitely not. So I guess that means you two are doing well?"

There was a long pause.

Too long.

"Silas?"

"I have something else to tell you."

"Okay . . ."

"You're not going to like it."

"Okay . . ."

"You may want to kick my ass."

I groaned. "Silas, please just tell me."

"Justin and I sort of . . . eloped."

My heartbeat thudded in my ears. I shook my head in confusion, my wine glass suspended halfway to my lips. I couldn't have heard that right. Silas—my commitment-phobic best friend—married? To someone he'd been dating for just a few months?

"Say something, love."

"I don't think I can."

"Shit, I'm sorry, Georgia. When we were in Mexico for spring break, it just happened. We were having such a great time; it was perfect. The sun was out, the water was warm, the bed was big. He just asked me and I said yes. We did it an hour later on the beach. I don't think he was expecting to do it. It just happened, Georgia, and I knew you would be pissed that I did it without you, but it felt so right," he finally finished.

"I . . . I don't even know what to say." I was still in shock. My brain wasn't computing what he was telling me.

"Congratulations, maybe?" Silas asked.

"God, I'm sorry. Congratulations. Of course,

congratulations. I'm thrilled for you. I'm sad I wasn't there, but I'm thrilled. Just shocked."

"I know. This doesn't seem like me, but Justin, he's—"

"He's perfect," I finished, a grin pulling at my cheeks. "God, Silas. You're married." Tears sprang to my eyes when I thought of my best friend finding someone he loved so completely that he promised to spend his life with him.

"I know." I could hear him tearing up on the other end. "You're making me cry, Georgia."

"I'm crying too." Emotion shook my body as tears streamed down my face. I wiped them with the back of one hand.

Tristan came up and wrapped both his arms around my body from behind. "Congrats, Silas," he muttered into the phone before tucking his face into my neck and kissing at the overheated flesh.

"Tell your hunk of a boyfriend thanks," Silas said.

"Hey, you're a taken man now." I laughed.

"Just 'cause I'm off the market doesn't mean I'm dead."

"Heard that." Tristan pulled his sensual lips from my neck and sang into the phone before attacking my lobe with his teeth.

"God, wait, you let me ramble on and on about my bullshit and here you'd gotten married, Silas?" I felt so selfish.

"You needed to get it out. I understand."

"It's not anywhere near as important as your news. You should have stopped me."

"It is important, love. But thanks. I love you."

"I love you, too." Another happy tear trickled down my cheek. Silas had been through so much over the years, been so ravaged by the pain and judgment put on him by his parents, it was overwhelming that he'd finally loved himself enough to give his heart to another. I wouldn't have thought it possible a year ago, but now, it did feel right.

"I'm going to let you get back to what you were doing. I can hear him sucking on you."

I laughed as tears rolled down my cheeks. "See you soon?"

"See you soon, love."

"Silas?"

"Yeah?"

"Congratulations again."

"Thanks," he murmured before hanging up the phone. I set my cell on the counter and spun around on the stool to land in Tristan's arms.

"I can't believe he got married."

"Why?" Tristan whispered as he made his way up the column of my neck, sucking on my flesh as he went. I arched away from him to get his attention.

"Because it's Silas. He's such a slut."

"*Was* a slut. Find the right person and suddenly it becomes not so hard to change your habits." He latched onto my neck and ran his hands up my shirt. His words didn't have time to resonate because he overwhelmed my body with his lips as I locked my arms around his neck and gave into his sensual assault.

Seventeen

Georgia

“This has got to stop, seriously.” Tristan arched one eyebrow at me as I sat curled in his lap on the couch watching *The Notebook* while a light spring rain pattered against the windows.

“What are you talking about?” I grinned up at him as he stroked his long fingers through my thick hair.

“I’m talking about the sappy shit. It’s got to end. I can’t take it for another minute.” He pushed himself off the couch and snagged the remote on his way.

“Hey! You can’t deprive me of Nick,” I screamed and darted for him as he flicked to an action movie.

“The sappy shit is only for girls who aren't getting any, and you’re getting it, right here.” He poked his thumb at his chest.

I rolled my eyes. “You are so full of yourself.”

“Call it like I see it.” He lifted one shoulder.

"So do I, and I'm callin' bullshit." I angled around a corner of the island in my quest to get the remote back.

"Oh, I don't think so." He walked backward with the sexiest smirk lighting his face. "I'm quite sure I keep you satisfied in all departments." He wiggled his eyebrows at me.

"You are so corny." I shook my head and lunged for the remote in his hands. He dropped it on the countertop and caught me in his arms, pulling me tight to his body and wrapping one warm palm around my neck. Leaning in, he took my lips in a predatory kiss. I moaned into his mouth and arched my body into him. I was putty in his hands. His lips, his deft fingers, that smile had me melting in a puddle at his feet and he knew it.

"You don't play fair." I pulled away from his lips.

"Playing fair is overrated. I know my talents and I use them to my advantage." He arched my neck to the side and sucked on the flesh. I moaned and savored his lips on my skin. "You're so beautiful, Georgia. Have I told you that? Because I need to each and every single day. You're so beautiful and I can't get enough of you."

I groaned in response as he pushed me back against the counter. I was pinned between the hard granite and the wall of his chest, and it was heaven. With one hand at the small of my back, he bent me backward and slid his hand up my chest and along my throat, arching my neck to reveal more flesh to him.

He trailed his lips along my skin and murmured, "I can't get enough of my lips on you. Tasting you. Exploring your beautiful body. I want to be inside you every day. I ache when we're apart."

"Oh God," I moaned and hooked my legs around his waist, pressing my body into his, rubbing and grinding, seeking relief from the tension that was building.

"Let's get married," he blurted as he ran a hand up and under my shirt.

"What?" My eyes fluttered open. I must have been hearing things. There was no way Tristan just asked me to marry him. Not after we'd only been together a few months. Not after we'd started out on such rocky ground.

"Marry me. I want you every single day for the rest of my life. My day isn't complete until I wake up to your beautiful face. Your smart mouth. I need it to keep me in line." A sexy smirk danced across his face.

"Okay, I agree with that last part, but are you nuts?" I shoved him off me.

"Head over heels for you," he murmured and sucked my earlobe into his mouth.

"Stop, you're trying to use your talents to sway me." I giggled and pushed him off me again.

"Whatever it takes, baby." He grinned unapologetically.

"I'm not marrying you."

I watched hurt flash across his eyes.

"I don't mean that. I mean, I'm not marrying you *now*."

"Why?" He watched me, the most endearing, perplexed look on his face, as if he really didn't understand why I would say no.

"I'll ask again: are you nuts?"

"I already told you, I'm head over heels for you. Completely drunk on you. If I know one thing for sure, it's that you and I are it. I told you—you own me." His voice lowered as he finished.

"I know, but—"

"No buts. It is what it is." He snaked his hands around my waist and pushed his hips into me. "Say no all you want, Georgia, but I'm not taking it back. You're mine."

"Are you saying this because you're worried because of the letter? Because I have to go back to DC?"

"No fucking way. Not even close. Don't read more into it than what it is. I want you, end of story."

"You always want me," I murmured, referring to his hard as steel erection pressed between us.

"No hiding it, no denying it." He dipped his head to catch my lips with his. "Come on. Silas and Justin tied the knot."

I heaved a sigh. "You are relentless."

"I like getting my way." He kissed me: exploring, tasting, owning. I popped the button on his jeans and slid them and his briefs over his thighs before I took his cock in my hand.

"I like getting my way too." I peered up at him from beneath my lashes before dropping down on my knees and lapping at his throbbing dick.

"Fuck." He sifted his hands through my hair as I worked up and down his length.

"Hands off," I instructed between licks. "Put them on the counter." This was about me being in control and denying him what he wanted.

Eighteen

Tristan

"Christ, Georgia," I groaned and clutched at the edge of the counter. She sucked so fucking hard, I thought my mind would explode. I wouldn't last more than a few more strokes, and I knew this was a power play on her part. She was trying to divert my mind from my impromptu proposal and fuck if it wasn't working. She did own me. And she was just proving that ten times over by dropping on her knees and putting her mouth on me.

"Fuck, I need to touch you," I moaned and threw my head back, the muscles taut in my throat, my breathing heavy, my chest wracked with desperate pants.

"Can't get everything you want," she mumbled around a mouthful of my dick.

"Fuck," I groaned as my hips thrust involuntarily into her face. My hands fisted around the countertop until my knuckles turned white. "You drive me insane," I gritted through my teeth. "My dick between your lips is a beautiful thing, but I need to come inside you." I threw caution to the wind and lifted her up to stand, yanked her pants down her legs and ran my fingers down her wet slit. "Turns you on sucking me off, hey, baby?"

"Yes . . ." she moaned, her beautiful body thrown back in pleasure. I ran my fingers between her lips and pulled at her swollen clit, causing her body to arch and buck into me before I thrust two fingers inside her.

"So fucking hot." I lifted her shirt with my other hand and ducked my head under the fabric to attach my lips to her nipple. I sucked and elongated the peak, kneading her flesh with my palm. I massaged circles around her clit with my thumb as I thrust my fingers in and out of her until I felt her body quiver and start the descent into falling apart. "Ah, not yet, beautiful." I pulled my fingers from her body and traced them up her neck to land at her full lips. "You're going to come with me inside you." I traced my fingers, wet from her juices, along her lips before plunging them into her mouth. Her eyes shot open and she sucked my fingers as tightly as she'd been sucking my cock just minutes ago. Her chocolate brown eyes peered up at me from beneath thick lashes, hooded and lustful, and driving me to fucking distraction. She looked so innocent, but that was the last thing she was. She embraced her sexuality completely and it was just another reason she owned me completely.

"You're fucking gorgeous." I pulled my fingers from her mouth and took her lips with mine, devouring her. Tasting her arousal on her lips had my dick rock-fucking-hard and ready to explode if I didn't get inside her beautiful body soon. I lifted her up on the counter and impaled her. Sheathed myself in her pulsing hot pussy and slammed back and forth.

I brought it straight fucking home because I didn't have the patience to wait. She was mine and she needed to know it. I had to show her. I took her head in both of my hands and thrust my tongue into her mouth, searching her and invading her just in the same way we were connected as I thrust my cock inside her. I wanted to crawl into her; it was fucking home to have her take me in this way, embracing me. I'd never felt so possessive and loved all in the same moment like I did when Georgia and I came together like this.

"Oh God, oh God, oh God," she groaned as her pussy clenched my cock like a fist and tremors wracked her body. Her eyes fluttered closed as her arms gave out and she crumpled back on the counter.

"Eyes, I want your eyes when I'm inside you." I ground my hips into her and circled them around, taking advantage of her orgasm to launch my own. My thighs clenched and my fingers dug into her soft hips as I poured myself into her. I wanted it all with her. My whole fucking future was laid at my doorstep as I revealed myself to her, opened up to her, and saw the next fifty years of our lives together. A white dress, kids, family vacations, a rocking chair on the very same deck of the house we were fucking in right now. I wanted it all and having it with anyone else other than the girl that'd just come undone underneath me wasn't an option. I just hoped she felt it too

Nineteen

Tristan

“I have to go. I promise I won't see him—I have no reason to, but I have to go.” Georgia sat beside me on the newly restored porch as we sipped coffee. Spring rain was misting down around us as we watched the waves roll in. Her first renters were scheduled for this weekend and she’d busted her ass for the last few weeks to get the house in perfect condition. She’d been a nervous wreck. And I’d suspected she'd thrown herself into the rental to forget the parole hearing that was fast approaching. Oh yeah, and that fucking proposal that we hadn’t talked about since it had happened. She’d done a stellar job distracting me with her lips around my dick, but don’t think it hadn’t crossed my mind since. It might have been in the moment and impulsive, a jackass move for me since I didn’t even have a ring for her, but if she would have said yes, I would have carried her off that same day and tied her to me, body and soul, forever.

“I get you have to go, but I don’t get why I can’t go with you.” I took a sip of my coffee as my eyes stayed trained on hers.

“I have to do this by myself. You don’t understand. Kyle was always there for me, through all of this, holding my hand. He was my lifeline. I need to be my own lifeline—strong enough to face this to get over it.” Her fingers stroked my hand sweetly.

"I get it, but I don't like it." I sighed. "How long will you be gone?" The parole hearing was next week and now that everything with the beach rental was taken care of, she had lots of excess energy to focus on it.

"A day or two tops."

"Can't Silas go with you?" If I couldn't be there, he would be the next best thing. I knew he wouldn't let anything happen to her.

"No, and anyway, he's busy. He and Justin are working on getting financing for the pub. Remember?"

Silas and Justin were trying to open a gastropub in downtown Wilmington. Justin had the culinary skills to feed the masses and Silas had the finances and energy to get it off the ground.

"I just don't want you facing it alone." I also didn't want her running into Kyle. I knew she wouldn't seek him out, but I didn't trust him not to pull shit if he heard she was in town. I also hated to admit in some deep, dark part of me, I was concerned she wouldn't be able to resist his advances and would fall back into old habits, just as she'd always done.

"I'll be fine." She leaned over and pecked me on the lips. She tasted like coffee and vanilla, just how she'd always tasted. That flavor had my heart racing since I'd tasted it on her lips last summer when we'd shared our first kiss. Vanilla had become synonymous with Georgia and it made me love her all the more.

Love.

I'd finally admitted it to myself. I'd been afraid to admit that before the proposal, but after, all bets were off. In my mind, anyway. I just needed to get past this parole hearing before I put us on the path to our future. Because the future was ours, our futures were forever entwined. I just had to show her that.

"Come here." I hauled her out of her chair and plopped her in my lap. She wrapped her arms around my shoulders and tucked her head into my neck. My heart skipped a few beats with her wrapped around me, just in the same way she was wrapped around my heart. If this girl left me again, she would crush me.

Completely.

"I love you." I held her cheeks in my hands and searched her eyes for something that would tell me she felt the same way.

Twenty

Georgia

He'd said it. He'd finally said the words we hadn't said to each other since my world had fallen apart last summer. He'd asked me to marry him this winter and yet we still hadn't said those words again. It didn't matter, because he'd settled into my heart and without saying the words, I knew I was his completely. I did love him, more than I ever thought it possible to love someone.

"I love you too," I whispered and pressed my lips to his, molding us together in a way that took my breath away. "I love you completely." I pulled away and held his face in mine. "And you don't have to worry. I feel okay with this. I'll be fine. I'm going in there, saying what I have to say, and leaving."

"Coming back to me?" His deep green eyes swam with emotion as he searched my face.

"Only place I wanna be is right here." I pressed my

hand to his chest, directly over his heart.

"Okay." He licked his lips as relief flooded his face. "I love you." His easy grin returned and his eyes did that beautiful sparkling thing that never failed to have me melting at his feet.

"I told you, I love you too." I grinned before crawling off his lap.

"Smart ass." He smacked me on the bottom before I swung around and headed back into the house. My heart was so light, it took my breath away. I'd needed time to process the upcoming parole hearing, but Tristan had helped me by getting on with our lives. We hadn't dwelled; he hadn't insisted we talk about it. I spoke about it when I wanted to, but he never pushed me. He held me when I woke up from a nightmare and shushed me back to sleep. It took time, but soon they dissipated.

I also came to the decision that I was ready to seek out a therapist in Wilmington. I didn't want to fall back into that dark place, and I couldn't expect Tristan, and shouldn't have expected Kyle, to save me from it. So I scheduled an appointment after I returned from DC and then sat down to write my letter to the parole board. I'd had a few dark moments; writing that letter felt a little like reliving the entire event, but when I put the letter down, I was able to move on. I was able to forget it. It was so easy to forget everything when I was wrapped in Tristan's arms.

The following week, I threw my purse in my car and wrapped myself around my beautiful boyfriend. I twisted my fingers in his golden-streaked hair and tried to reassure him with my lips that I would be back just as soon as the hearing was over. He'd grown increasingly anxious the week leading up to this moment, but he had to know he had nothing to fear.

"I'll see you in a few days." I traced the sharp angle of his jaw with the pad of my thumb. "Behave yourself."

"Always." He crooked a grin at me. "Charlie and I have male bonding to do."

"Don't forget Diva," I pouted.

"She'll keep us in line."

"I'm sure she will." I patted his cheek and then pressed my lips back to his. I didn't want to leave him here. A huge part of my heart wanted to haul him along with me, his hand wrapped in mine every step of this horrific process, but I had to prove to myself that I could tackle this on my own. I didn't need anyone; I was determined to come face to face with my past and conquer it.

"I love you, Georgia," he murmured.

"I love you too," I whispered as we pulled apart, our arms stretched and hands locked, before they finally dropped to our sides and I crawled into the front seat of my car and backed down the driveway of our little home.

Dressed in a power suit and black patent heels to give myself a boost of confidence, I pulled into a parking spot outside the Department of Corrections building and spotted a familiar face.

"You've got to be kidding me," I mumbled as I stepped out of my car. "What are you doing here?" I glared as Kyle stepped up to me.

"I'm here for you," he answered as he pulled me into an awkward hug.

"How did you know this was happening today?" I pulled away from him.

"You got a letter at the apartment. I had it forwarded, didn't you notice it said so on the envelope?"

"I guess not," I mumbled. My mind had gone on meltdown as soon as I'd seen the return address; nothing else had registered.

"I don't need you here." I instantly felt terrible for pushing Tristan away from today, insisting I do it myself, and yet here stood Kyle. It would tear Tristan up if he knew.

"Of course you do. You need someone, and since it looks like you're solo . . ." He trailed off with an arched eyebrow.

"Tristan wanted to come. I told him he couldn't."

"Well, either way, I'm glad you're not alone for this." He locked my hand in his own.

"I can handle this, Kyle." I jerked my hand away from him. "I've got to get in there," I mumbled as I took long strides away from him.

"I'm not letting you go in there alone, Georgia. No matter what you think, you need someone, and I'm just glad I made the decision I did to come today, considering you've been left alone by the person who you think cares so much about you."

"He respects me," I mumbled as I kept walking, Kyle hustling behind me. I hurried up the few steps and opened the door of the brick building. We made our way through security before stepping up to the receptionist's desk.

"I'm here for a parole hearing." I passed the letter I'd received through the window. The receptionist scanned the letter and then looked up at me and over to Kyle.

"I'm her lawyer." He pressed a hand to the small of my back. I shot him a glare as a shiver ran down my spine from his touch. She finally nodded before sending another guard out to escort us to the parole board meeting room.

Thirty minutes later, the hearing was over. I'd read my letter, teared up repeatedly, before breaking down completely. My shoulders were hunched and trembling as Kyle rubbed my back and whispered in my ear that it was going to be okay. Looks of sympathy spread across the parole board's faces as they watched me pour my heart out to them. Perfect strangers who held the stability of my future in their hands. Emotions seeped through me because it felt like my parents' memory, the tragic way they'd ended, how the world would perceive their story, was held in the hands of these half a dozen strangers. As we stepped out of the room, we passed a middle-aged woman with someone who looked to be her son. He looked no more than eighteen years old and was a perfect image of his father, the man that had taken my parents' lives and had set me on a path full of pain. I paused for a moment when I looked into the woman's eyes. She was teary and worn, as if she'd lived a hard life. I'm sure she had, and I felt badly for her. I felt an odd sense of kinship with her. Our lives had both been vaulted down a painful path through no fault of our own. The men who'd entered my house that night had taken things from both of us, things we could never get back.

I swallowed back another sob as Kyle wrapped an arm

around my waist and pulled me into him.

We reached the open air of the parking lot and I sucked in deep breaths.

"You okay?" He rubbed my back.

"I'm fine. I'm glad this is behind me. My part of it, anyway." We wouldn't know the parole board's decision for up to a month and even then, I would be notified by letter.

"Do you want to get something to eat?" He continued to soothe me, rubbing my back, up my neck, down to the hollow of my spine, nearly to the top of my ass.

"Look, Kyle, I'm glad you were here. It was sweet of you. But none of this is a good idea. Us being together; it's just not good," I murmured. I had another night reserved at the hotel, but all I could think about was getting home to Tristan and our little slice of heaven on the beach.

"Is that your opinion or his?" His eyes flashed in anger.

"Mine," I said firmly as I opened my car door.

"Look, Georgia. We've got a lot of history. Let me just take you out for something to eat. I wouldn't want you driving while you're so upset anyway. I already have reservations."

"Kyle," I groaned.

"Come on. I'll drive and bring you back to your car when we're done."

I heaved a big sigh before caving. "Fine," I murmured

as I crawled into his black Audi. I knew Tristan wouldn't approve, but Kyle and I had grown up together, we had so much history, I wanted some sense of closure between us. I hated that the last time I'd seen him fists had been thrown.

A few minutes later, we pulled up to the Italian bistro we used to frequent. It was small, the lights were dim, the setting intimate and romantic.

"Really, Kyle?" I cocked an eyebrow at him.

"Can't blame me for trying." He passed me a sheepish grin.

"I can, actually. I'm with someone and I love him."

"Okay. It's just lunch, though." He patted my knee like a big brother would. He was all over the place today and consequently had me unsure of whether I was coming or going.

Kyle escorted me into the restaurant by the small of my back before we sat down in a private corner. The hum of conversation was low around us. Kyle placed our orders. He remembered my favorites, and ordered a bottle of wine. This was all becoming very date-like and making my stomach twist with anxiety.

"Look, Georgia, I know you're happy. You seem happy —happy as I've ever seen you, and I know it wasn't me that did that. I haven't put that smile on your face in years, and I feel terrible about that." Kyle sipped his wine as his deep chocolate brown eyes bore into mine.

I took a drink and let the liquid ease down my throat, tingle out across my shoulders, and relax my whole body. "It's okay, no apologies. It's all in the past."

"I know, but the thing is, I don't want it to be. I miss you like fucking crazy. I fucked up so much, and I don't blame you for leaving me, but I want you to know it's the best thing you could have done. I know that now. I've learned a lot—came to a lot of realizations. You were my everything, Georgia, and I took advantage of that, but I won't anymore. I've changed." He grabbed my hand and caressed the palm with his fingers. "Believe me, I've changed, and if you'd just give me another chance," he whispered as his gaze held mine.

"This isn't what I came here for, Kyle." I pulled my hand from his and brought my wine glass to my lips again.

"I know. I know you think you and he are good together, but remember, Georgia. We were great. We were something. We were perfect for so long. I want that back. I'm going to make us work. No more fucking around, I swear. Just give me the chance to prove it to you."

His beautiful browns held mine and I got lost in who we used to be. My memory drifted down the path to our past: high school, summers with baseball games and Fourth of July fireworks, holding hands and laughing, and it was all so sweet and fun until real life interceded and we slowly became incompatible. Kyle needed something from me that I couldn't give him—mainly a trophy wife that would shut her mouth while he worked long hours and fucked his receptionist.

"I'm not what you need. Not anymore."

The waiter set our plates down and nodded before walking away, sensing the tension between us.

"I wish you wouldn't say that. I miss you so much. I need you. I love you. I couldn't ever love anyone like I love you," he murmured, looking as sad as I'd ever seen him. My heart cracked open just a little bit for him as I realized my mind was made up and he really didn't have a chance. Not with me, anyway.

"Look, Kyle, what we had was perfect for a while. It was beautiful and you were my everything, but that wasn't right for me. I have to be *my* everything, not someone else's. I need to put me first, and I'm doing that now." I stroked his forearm. He nodded solemnly before finally breaking my gaze and lifting his fork. We ate in silence the rest of the meal, and in some ways, it was more therapeutic than I ever imagined it could be.

We walked out of the restaurant an hour later, Kyle's hand at my back, leading me toward his car. We turned the corner of the building and approached his Audi to find a blonde in a too short dress, ankles crossed, ridiculously high heels on, leaning against the driver's side of his car.

"Sorry to interrupt your romantic interlude, but when you missed the baby appointment today, I checked your datebook to find you had a reservation here." The blonde sneered.

"Jesus Christ, Rachel." Kyle ran a shaky hand through his hair.

"Georgia, I assume?" She nodded at me, contempt clear in her eyes.

"This isn't what you think." Kyle dropped his hand from my back and looked between us. I wasn't sure which one of us he was talking to.

"Baby?" I arched an eyebrow at Kyle.

"I'm Rachel." The blonde stepped up to me and thrust a hand in my face. "His fiancée." She wiggled a rock in my face. "And mother of his child." She rubbed the small bump at her stomach.

"Baby, Kyle? Really? You've got a baby on the way?" I was so dumbfounded I couldn't think to say anything else. "And what was all that in there?" A grin split out across my face. His eyes narrowed at my reaction.

"Georgia, what I said, I meant."

"Oh, I'm sure you did. As sincere as ever, huh, Kyle? I came today to give you a chance to be civil. I hated that we ended so disastrously, but this Kyle, this is so wrong. I'm done trying to patch up any bad blood between us." I glared before glancing back at Rachel. "I'm sorry you're in the position you're in with him. I don't know you, but I know you deserve better. No girl deserves to be lied to. I just hope he's a better father than a fiancé," I spat before turning on my heel and heading back to the entrance of the restaurant to hail a taxi.

"What the fuck, Kyle?" I heard Kyle's baby momma shriek.

"Ow," Kyle groaned. She must have smacked him, and, without a doubt, he deserved it, that and much more. I laughed when I heard him trying to defend himself. This night had turned out much more entertaining than I'd originally thought it would be.

Twenty-One

Georgia

It was mid-afternoon when I left the restaurant. After getting my car and things from the hotel room, I checked out and hit the expressway, pushing the speed limit to get back to the beach and Tristan. He wasn't expecting me until tomorrow, but I couldn't stand the thought of spending another night in DC, hundreds of miles away from him and his comforting arms. I stopped for a triple shot latte for brain fuel and thought about calling him to let him know I'd be home early, but frowned when I found the battery on my phone had died. I tossed it on the seat beside me and continued to drive, music turned up, my foot edging the pedal a little more with every mile I passed, anxious to get home to my beautiful and supportive boyfriend. I wanted to be nowhere else except wrapped up in his strong arms. I wanted to peel my clothes off and lie against his chest, have him stroke my hair and wrap myself around his lean body and listen to his heartbeat as we fell asleep in our own little world.

I pulled onto our road after eight. It was normally a six-hour trip, but I'd made it in four and a half. I pulled into the twisting driveway and arched an eyebrow at the navy blue SUV parked next to Tristan's Jeep. I hadn't seen it before, maybe it was a neighbor, although I couldn't imagine who. I stepped out of the car, the waves crashing a little louder than usual, and saw Charlie trot around the side of the house. I bent and gave him a scratch behind the ear; he was as happy as ever to see me and get some attention.

"Hey, boy, is he outside with you?" Charlie gave his tail a wag and followed me as I made my way around the side of the house. I inhaled a deep breath of the uncharacteristically warm ocean air. I couldn't be happier to be back. The only thing that could make me happier would be Tristan's arms wrapped around me, soothing away the stress of this awful day.

I stepped around the corner and found Tristan facing away from me, leaning against the railing of the deck, a pair of long, bronzed, decidedly feminine arms wrapped around his neck. Bile jumped into my throat and my heart felt like it would thud straight out of my chest. He knew I was coming home tonight, so why was he here with someone else? Did he want me to find out? Did he want to get caught cheating?

Shock cemented me to my spot, my eyes staring, wide as saucers, as I watched the scene in front of me. The waves roared while my heart echoed erratically in my ears. I couldn't hear, I couldn't focus; all I could see was that nightmare playing out before me. The man I loved, in the embrace of another woman.

I thought I would faint.

I'd put everything I had into him. My trust, love, honesty, we'd started out so recklessly, our hearts on the line all last summer. I'd held out hope that we were in a better place, a place where we wouldn't do that to each other. Not after all we'd been through. But I should have known better. He'd been a whore, and he'd paraded his whores around me knowing he was hurting me, and here he was doing it again.

"Come on, I've missed you," I heard the beautiful blonde in his arms pout as she trailed a hand down to grab his ass and rub her body against his seductively. His hand lifted slowly and landed on her arm.

My stomach twisted painfully. So this was what it felt like to be cheated on. This was what it felt like when the one you loved was unfaithful, the evidence right here in my face. It was gut wrenching. The world felt like it was slipping away. My vision tunneled to their two bodies pressed together.

Charlie wagged his tail at my leg, unaware that my world was falling apart in the sand at my feet.

"You need to leave. I'm not telling you again; it's time for you go, Briana. I don't know how you found me out here, because I know I sure as shit didn't tell you where I was, but don't come back. Delete my number from your phone while you're at it," I heard Tristan growl. Confusion twisted my face before I watched him unlink her hands from around his neck and push her body away from him. Anger registered on her face as she glanced over his shoulder, a sneer registering when her eyes locked on mine.

"Her again? You're with her?"

Tristan's head whipped around and fear crossed his features. Our eyes met and the only sound that echoed around us was the waves hitting the shore. I pressed my lips together nervously. I wanted desperately to tear my eyes away from his, but I couldn't. I was pulled to him.

"Get the fuck out," he said, without tearing his eyes from mine. She smirked and stepped off the steps, brushing against my shoulder roughly as she walked past. "Georgia," he breathed as he hustled down the steps and then froze inches away from my body, looking as if he wanted to touch me, but wasn't sure how his touch would be received.

"That wasn't what it looked like. Christ, I know it

looked fucking terrible." He ran a nervous hand through his hair. "But I swear to you—"

"I know." I heaved a sigh and stepped into him.

He froze, arms at his sides. "Really?" he finally asked.

"Yeah." I breathed him in before wrapping my arms around his neck, tangling my fingers in his hair and nuzzling into the skin at his shoulder.

"God." The air released from his lungs in a whoosh before he wrapped his arms around me, holding me so tightly to his body it was like he wanted to meld us together. Like he wanted nothing between us, to make sure I was real, still standing here after what I'd just witnessed.

"I heard what you told her."

"I'm sorry." He threaded his fingers in my hair and held me tighter to him.

"Don't be. Although I hate that she knows where we live. And that she had her hands all over my man." I grinned and tugged at his hair playfully.

"Possessive, huh?" His beautiful smirk lit his lips.

"Very." I leaned up on tiptoes and kissed it off his lips.

"Tell me about your day." Tristan dusted his long fingers around the bare skin of my back. I was draped across his naked chest, my head resting over his heart, sucking in his fresh ocean scent mixed with the scent of our lovemaking. We lay with only a thin sheet covering our lower halves as we enjoyed the post-sex glow.

"It was awful. I'm glad it's over and I'm glad I'm home with you." I kissed his dark nipple and felt a shiver run across his body.

"Mmm, I'm glad you're home too." His voice was rough and sexy and had desire shooting tingles across my body.

"You miss me?"

"Just your sexy ass. I could do without the nagging." He smacked my bottom so hard it left a sting.

"What?" I squealed and pushed off of him, rubbing my ass. "I don't nag." I shot him a glare to see his sensual lips curved up in a mischievous smile.

"I know; I'm just kidding. I missed you. And this ass." He stroked his palm over my bottom softly.

"Good." I kissed his full lips before leaning back down on his chest.

"I'm glad you did it alone, baby. I get it now."

"Mmm, I wasn't alone," I whispered as a sleepy haze infiltrated my brain.

"What do you mean? Who was with you?" he murmured in my hair.

"I'll tell you in the morning. Too tired." I yawned and tucked into his neck, falling asleep to his delicate fingers running figure eights around my back.

Twenty-Two

Tristan

"Hey, babe?" I stepped up behind her as she made coffee, her first morning home.

"Yeah?" she turned and planted a kiss on my lips. "Good morning."

"I guess so." I slid my palms up under her shirt and pulled her hips to mine. "Very good morning." I caught her lips in a kiss and thrust my tongue in her mouth, devouring her first thing. Best morning ritual ever. I skimmed my hand up her narrow waist and palmed her tits in my hands, pinching her nipples just to hear her squeal.

"That hurts," she squeaked, but her lips landed back on mine again.

"I thought you liked it when I was rough?" I murmured between kisses.

"Mmm, I do . . ." she moaned and arched into me. I slid one hand down inside her little sleep shorts, the ones that drove me insane because she looked so hot in them. I ran my fingers down the crack of her ass and pressed her to me, sliding my fingers through her wet folds from behind. "Jesus," she moaned as I swirled a fingertip around her swollen flesh.

"Fuck. Wet first thing in the morning? I think you were made for me." I thrust a finger inside her and pumped as she arched and moaned into my mouth.

"Tristan, oh God," she panted before I felt her tight walls quiver and clench around my fingers. An orgasm shot through her body and sent waves of pleasure coursing from head to toe. Her head fell onto my shoulder and her legs went limp. She rested against me, her breaths coming out heavy and erratic.

"God, how can you just do that first thing?" she murmured sleepily.

"I've got great inspiration." I kissed along the flesh of her neck, goose bumps pebbling in my wake. It felt good that her body was so attuned to mine. I had the same effect on her she had on me.

"You make me feel . . . you know just how to . . . God, you own my body," she finally completed her thought.

I chuckled and sucked her earlobe into my mouth. "Don't forget it, baby."

"So, what were you going to ask me?" She plopped down in a deck chair a few minutes later, a steaming cup of coffee in her hands.

"Before I made you come so hard you nearly fell at my feet?" I shot her that smile reserved only for her.

"Yeah, that." She rolled her eyes.

"You said you weren't alone yesterday. Did Silas come up after all?"

"Oh, no." She took a sip of her coffee as if she were avoiding answering me. "Kyle was there."

I narrowed my eyes at her, my jaw working back and forth as I tried to process the information. She hadn't let me go with her, and her ex-fucking-boyfriend had shown up? "Why didn't you tell me?"

"I didn't mean to not tell you; I was just so tired, and after what I came home to . . ." she said, referring to finding Briana plastered all over my body on the back porch. Georgia ran a nervous fingertip around the lip of her cup. I gritted my teeth together. I was trying to think this through, trying to contain the anger, trying not to jump to conclusions and lash out.

It wasn't working.

"That's fucking bullshit, Georgia."

"What?" She whipped her head to me in confusion.

"You wouldn't let me go with you, and I wanted to,

begged you to let me go, and then he goes with you anyway? What else happened? What else aren't you telling me? And don't use last night as an excuse because you knew nothing happened with Briana and me. You were there when I pushed her away." I knew I was losing it, letting my temper take over, but I couldn't help it. It ripped me up inside that Kyle, the douchebag who had cheated on her for years, had been there for her and I hadn't. Maybe I should have insisted on going anyway, regardless of what she had thought. Lesson fucking learned.

"What are you talking about? Don't be like that. I'm not *not* telling you anything. I didn't get a chance." Her features pressed into a hard line and I knew she was pissed. This day was only going downhill and I should have known after the fantastic orgasm I'd given her this morning that it was the only way to go.

"It's pretty fucking suspicious you won't let me go, but then he shows up to save the day, just like he's always done. When he wasn't fucking around on you, that is."

Her mouth dropped open in a perfect O and I knew I'd gone too far. Anger and pain flashed across her beautiful, sad eyes before she jumped out of the chair and bee-lined for the house. I followed her in, hot on her heels, begging her to stop and hear me out, before she stomped into our room and slammed the door full force in my face. Another inch and she would have smashed my nose.

She was pissed.

But still so fucking hot with all that rage boiling up inside of her. What the fuck was wrong with me—Georgia mad gave me a hard-on?

I ran a hand through my hair and heaved a sigh.

"Look, Georgia, I'm sorry. I didn't mean what I said. I shouldn't have said it. I'm an asshole."

"Fuck, yeah, you are," I heard her growl on the other side of the door. It sounded like she was standing right there. A fist clenched around my heart at the pain in her voice.

"I'm sorry. Will you open the door and talk to me?" I whispered, my palm splayed across the wood of the door.

"No," she yelled.

"Please?"

"No. Go away." I heard the lock click into place.

"Fuck, come on, Georgia, I'm trying. Just give me a chance," I said softly. She didn't answer, so I took it as an invitation to continue. "I just . . . flipped when you said his name. I knew he would try to get you back. I'm kicking myself for not going. I should have been there for you, no matter what you said. Christ, I could've sat in the car if you'd wanted me to, but I would have been there. It killed me to let you go alone. And then he shows up . . ." I trailed off, my thoughts a confused blur in my head.

I heard the latch unlock and the door creaked open. Her beautiful brown eyes stared back at me, wet and swirling with emotion.

"Christ, don't cry. I never want to make you cry, Georgia." I barged through the small crack she'd left me and wrapped her in my arms. Sobs overtook her body and we sank to the floor, her legs wrapped around my waist, my hands locked around her back. Her body trembled in my arms.

"It was so hard, being there. Confronting it, then I ran into his family in the hallway. I felt so bad for them. They were me. They were as innocent as I was, as my parents were. They were victims too. Then I felt terrible for begging the parole board not to let him out, because I was taking him away from his family, another family ruined. My family had already been taken away from me. It seemed wrong to make another one suffer."

"No, Georgia, no, no. He did that. He chose that; that's not on you," I murmured as I stroked the thick mane of hair that fell down her back.

"I know he chose it, but it's been fifteen years; maybe he served his time," she whimpered.

"Well, that's up to them, baby. They'll know what to do. You did what you felt was right in here." I pointed at her heart. "Now it's up to them to do what's right up here." I pointed at my head. "It's over. Whatever happens, it's over for you."

She nodded and hiccupped softly.

"I'm sorry I didn't tell you sooner about Kyle. He took me out to eat, he tried to get me back, but then we ran into his baby mama slash fiancée. I took a taxi back to my car and all I could think about was getting back to you." She said all of this in a rush between hiccups.

"Christ." My brain swirled with the new information. That fucking douchebag had a fiancée and a baby on the way and he was trying to get my girl back?

"It's okay. I know you didn't get a chance to tell me last night. I shouldn't have reacted how I did. My brain just went haywire when you said he was with you. But I know nothing happened. Not that I trust him a fucking inch, but I trust you." I wrapped my hands around her neck and caressed the smooth curve of her jaw line. "And, just for the record, he's a douche for moving on so quickly. I could never, if we didn't work—" I couldn't finish that thought. "It would destroy me. That's all. I'm sorry you invested so many years being with him, and then he could just do that . . ." I trailed off.

"It doesn't even matter. I just feel bad for her. And terrible for their baby. Kyle used to be a good guy. I just hope he can be a good father. Every baby deserves a good dad." Sadness washed over her face and I sensed something more she wasn't telling me.

"Are you sad he's starting a family without you?" The question fucking hurt, and I wasn't sure I wanted the answer, but I had to ask.

"No." She shook her head. "It's not that, just mourning the loss of what I thought my life would be. Do you know what I mean?"

"I guess." I didn't, because I'd never had a plan for my life, never cared to have one until she breezed into it and swept the air straight out of my lungs.

"I'm not mourning the loss of him or my relationship with him. It's just the plan I had for my life is different now. It's so much better; I'm so much better." She grabbed my face between her palms and stroked my cheeks with the pads of her thumbs. "But it's still an adjustment. I feel a little off kilter, you know?" She continued to soothe me with the soft timbre of her voice, her soothing touch on my skin.

"Yeah." I pressed a kiss on her lips.

"I love you, Tristan. You're not getting rid of me so easily." She gave a soft tug on my hair and then wrapped her arms around me, pressing our bodies flush, relieving the tension that had settled in my muscles.

"I love you too," I muttered and relished in the feel of her body pressed to mine. The girl could turn me from a bear to a puppy dog in an instant with just her touch.

Twenty-Three

Georgia

"Mmm, where are you going?" his sleepy voice grumbled as he wrapped an arm around my waist and locked me to him.

"It's the big day; I've go a lot to do." I giggled when he thrust his hips into mine, giving me a clear indication of his morning erection.

"Let's stay in bed all day. I want you to myself. I'm sick of sharing." He pouted before sucking the flesh along my neck. His palm skated up my torso to palm my breast and pinch my nipple, a zing of delicious pleasure shooting straight to my core.

"You want me all to yourself every day." I nipped at his lip, causing his hips to thrust into mine again. He snaked a hand around and held both my ass cheeks in his hands tightly, pressing me firmly to him so I could feel every glorious inch of his body.

"You have to let me go," I murmured as my eyes fluttered closed. I relished his smooth skin against mine.

"Never."

"But if you don't, I'll give in," I moaned, because I was already giving in.

"My plans are working, then."

"They always do."

"Not as often as I'd like." He smacked my ass.

"Twice a day not enough for you?" I rolled my eyes.

"Don't get smart with me." He grabbed my chin and pulled my lips to his, capturing me in a rough kiss. He was taking possession, proving my body was his, but he didn't need to, because I already knew it and was a willing participant. I'd always been unable to resist his charms, and he used that against me on a daily basis.

I crawled up his body and straddled his hips, my hands cupping his face, my dark hair curtaining around us as we devoured each other. Tasting and licking, moaning and sucking.

"Christ, you're going to kill me." He dashed forward and snagged my bottom lip between his teeth and bit almost painfully. I giggled and fell back on the bed. His strong arms caged me in as his eyes sparkled with mischief and desire.

He was beautiful.

And always so playful.

It was what had me falling so hard from the beginning, the piece of him that had brought the light back to my life. He was my light in the darkness.

"Death by sex; you'd love it." I indulged in one long kiss before pushing him off me.

"I can think of no better time to die, than buried deep inside you." His lips turned up in a cocky smirk.

"Tristan." My mouth dropped open in shock. "You can't say stuff like that." I turned and headed for the en suite bathroom.

"Why? Does it make you wet?" His eyes were still doing that delicious sparkling thing I loved so much.

"Oh my God." I rolled my eyes. "I'm taking a shower."

"Can I come too?" He looked at me with the most endearing puppy dog eyes.

"You're ridiculous." I grinned. "No funny stuff." I pointed at him. His eyes lit up as he darted off the bed and lunged for me. I shrieked and made it into the bathroom before his arms locked around my waist.

"A shower without funny stuff doesn't sound like fun." He nipped at my earlobe.

"I mean it. The caterer's going to be here in an hour to set up. Hopefully it's not too windy out there today. If we fuck this up because of your overactive libido, Silas will kill both of us."

"My overactive libido? I'd argue that it's both of us." His lips were still attached to my earlobe as his hands were skimming across my body.

"Whatever, you horn dog. Shower?" I pushed him off me.

His eyes twinkled and a flirty grin lifted his lips. "Shower." He nodded, then stepped into the shower and began adjusting the water temperature. Not only did he have the body of a Greek fucking god, but his smile, his eyes, and his laugh lit my life. I'd made some poor decisions last summer, but I was just thankful I'd ended up on the right path, the path that had brought me right here, with him.

We sat at a round white linen-covered table on the beach, nestled in a nook among the sloping dunes between my rental house and Tristan's. Silas and Justin faced the roaring ocean waves, and we sat around them, celebrating their union. After Silas and Justin had gotten married this spring, I'd begged them to let me throw a reception. Silas had refused at every point, but I'd finally worn him down.

The early May temperatures were ideal; the slightest breeze blew and rustled the dune grass. The weather wasn't too hot or humid, and everything was perfect for our small gathering. Drew sat beside me, beautiful and glowing in a plum maternity dress. She was as big as a house and never stopped complaining about it, but Gavin doted on her, and took her bitchy attitude with a grain of salt. In fact, he was looking at her with as much love in his eyes as he'd had when they'd broken the news to us eight months ago. She was due at the end of this month, just over three weeks to go, and while she wasn't supposed to be traveling so far from home and her doctor, she'd refused to miss this. Deep down she loved Silas; she just didn't like to admit it.

Gavin sat next to her, a heavy arm wrapped around her shoulders, caressing the bare skin of her arm. She turned and laughed at something he said and then pecked him on the lips. I could see happiness dancing in their eyes, and the only thing that made me sad was that they lived so far away.

Justin's parents sat beside Justin. They looked just like him and were so sweet and supportive. Silas had married into a loving family and I couldn't have been happier. He'd never had that; I'd been his only family for so long. He deserved to know what love and acceptance felt like. Justin's parents were also happy because Silas and Justin had set up their permanent residence near them. I was overjoyed that Silas would be less than a half hour from me. Life was finally falling into place.

"A toast to the beautiful couple." Tristan raised his glass and everyone followed suit. "I would, without a doubt, be wildly jealous of another man cuddling with my girl on the couch watching sappy chick flicks, but thankfully, Silas likes boys, so as long as I don't have to watch those movies with her . . ." I trailed off as I winked at Georgia. She rolled her eyes back at me. "In all seriousness, Justin and Silas, you both deserve all the happiness in the world. Everyone deserves to find their other half, and I know both of you will cherish the love you've found for a lifetime." I paused as soft clapping sounded around the table. "And a toast to the beautiful hostess. The last year has been the best of my life because you've been in it, Georgia. We didn't always do things in a conventional way, and our love didn't take a natural path, but it took the one it needed to take, and I'm just glad that my path led me here with you." He stood and I raised my eyes at him in question. He pulled my chair out to face him before he dropped down on one knee and reached into the pocket of his dress pants.

"The last year you've made me so much happier than I could have ever imagined being. You bring light to my life in a way I never thought possible. I want to spend my life with you, wake up to you, fall asleep with you, fall asleep *in* you," he murmured the last part under his breath. My cheeks flushed as a smile tugged at my lips. "I want to give you everything, experience everything with you. I want babies and minivans and family vacations and Christmases. I want to spend my life giving you everything you deserve. Will you spend yours with me?" Emotion swirled in his deep green orbs and I forgot to breathe. Once again, he took my breath away. He kept me on my toes and had me smiling and laughing more than anyone ever had. I loved every minute of it and I loved my life with him.

I nodded and sucked in a sharp breath. Mist fogged my vision. I laughed nervously, trying to hold back the tears.

"Will you marry me, Georgia?"

"Yes." I nodded and lunged into his arms. He locked me in his embrace and held me so tightly I could barely breathe. He consumed me. I inhaled his scent and my eyes fluttered closed. I was as happy as I'd ever been.

"Let me get this ring on your finger." Tristan pulled away and slipped a large cushion-cut diamond with pave diamonds surrounding the center and the sides on my finger. It was stunning. He'd chosen a ring that left me breathless, just like he did, every day.

Cheers and claps from our little group erupted.

"A toast for the newly engaged couple," Justin sang as he lifted his glass. Everyone toasted around us. Tristan stood and lifted me with him. I was too scared to let go of him. Too scared that this couldn't be real, couldn't be my life.

"I'm so happy for you, love." Silas leaned over and planted a kiss on my cheek when I sat down.

"Did you know?" My teary eyes searched my best friend's.

He nodded with a small smile. "He asked me."

My heart cracked and love filled it even further. Tristan had asked Silas if he could marry me. I couldn't even put into words how much that meant to me. My parents had been stolen from me and Silas was the only family I'd had for a long time. Tristan knew and respected that. The gesture alone clearly showed the love he had for me. How much he *got* me.

"You deserve beautiful, love." Silas pulled my head into him, our foreheads pressed together and tears falling down my cheeks.

"You do too," I murmured.

"I've got it," he whispered and pecked me on the lips.

"I love you, Silas."

"I love you too." He kissed me on the tip of the nose before pulling away. I swallowed the lump in my throat and then turned back to Tristan. The love pooling in his eyes made me smile. He rested a warm hand on my thigh and squeezed. A little gesture to let me know he knew and understood. A sign that the love he had for me was even more than I had imagined. From the moment we’d met, our paths had been leading us here, regardless of what we'd wanted. It’d been inevitable.

“I love you,” I whispered.

“I love you so much more.” He snagged my chin and planted a kiss on my lips. A grin broke out across my face as I shut my eyes.

“Thank you.” I meant for everything. For putting up with all we’d been through last summer and the indecision that had me torn every which way. For taking me back, for loving me, for asking me to marry him, for accepting me, for accepting my friends. For all of it.

“No problem,” he whispered as his lips lifted in a breathtaking smile.

Twenty-Four

Georgia

"I've got an appointment. Do you want me to pick anything up for dinner?"

"What kind of appointment?" Tristan's eyebrows knit together. He sat in his office chair, laptop open before him, fingers hovering over the keys.

"Therapy."

"Yeah?" He pushed the chair away from his desk and held his arms open. "Come here."

I stepped up to him and he wrapped his arms around my waist, fingers tracing small circles at the base of my spine. I threaded my fingers through his tousled hair; I think it soothed me as much as it helped to soothe him. "I did some research into alternative therapies. I've seen a therapist before, but it never really seemed to help much. There's a guy at the University of North Carolina who practices a new type of therapy, focusing less on feelings and more on happy memories, accepting the past to live in the present. My appointment's at one," I finished softly.

"That's great, baby," he murmured before he lifted the hem of my shirt and placed a soft kiss on my belly.

"I'm excited. I just . . . need to do something. After last summer, I . . . I need to stop being tied to the past. I need to find a better way to live," I murmured.

"Anything I can do?" His beautiful green eyes turned up to me.

"Whatever you've been doing is perfect." I leaned down and pressed my lips to his in a kiss. He groaned and pulled me into his lap, my legs dangling over his knees. He traced his hands up under the hem of my shirt and up the length of my spine.

"Sure you don't have five minutes?" he murmured before swiping one palm around the front of my ribcage and palming my breast through my bra.

"You're a five-minute man now?" I teased while nipping his bottom lip.

"I can make it work," he growled and tugged the cup of my bra down to take my nipple between his thumb and finger. He pulled and I arched into his body with a moan.

"Have to go," I breathed as my eyes fluttered closed.

"Five minutes." He lifted my shirt and dipped his head under the thin cotton to attach his lips to my nipple. He sucked and pulled on the pebbled peak until my blood was rushing through my veins and my core was wet with desire.

"Mmm, Tristan," I moaned as his other hand popped the button of my jeans and snaked inside my panties.

"You're so fucking wet, baby," he murmured before his lips attached to my other nipple and his long fingers caressed my aching center. He ran a finger between my lips and stroked between my thighs slowly, driving me to the brink of frustration. My heart thudded as I rocked my hips into him.

"I have to go," I moaned with no meaning whatsoever.

"Let me get you off."

"Tristan," I whimpered.

"I'm doing my part to relax you," he said before two fingers plunged into me. I sucked in a sharp breath and bit my lip between my teeth. "Let me hear you." He pumped his fingers in and out, hooking them to reach that delicious spot just inside.

"Fuck . . ." I moaned as he thrust and my hips worked back and forth on his palm.

"Love that dirty mouth, beautiful." He added a third finger and his thumb worked deliciously slow circles over my clit. Pleasure built between my thighs and my mind swam in a haze of lust-filled confusion. I rocked my hips into him, grinding my pelvis, seeking more. More everything. More friction. More pleasure. More him. My brain was chasing the orgasm that loomed seconds away.

"Fuck, God, Tristan," I panted and moaned before lightning sparks exploded behind my eyes and shivers raced through my body. My toes clenched, and my blood pumped through every vein I had as I pulsed around his fingers.

"God, you're fucking beautiful when you come all over my hand," he growled as he eased his fingers out of me and thrust one into his mouth. My eyes widened in surprise as he licked it clean. "Your fucking taste . . . I could never live without it."

My eyes flashed with desire. He cocked his beautiful head to one side, a soft lock of golden-blond hair falling across his forehead. He arched an eyebrow before sliding his palm over my collarbone, up my neck, cupping my cheek, and thrusting one finger, drenched with my juices, into my mouth. I closed my lips around his finger and sucked, never breaking eye contact with him.

"Jesus Christ," he breathed as his eyes watched my lips, wrapped around his finger. "You drive me fucking insane." He pulled his finger from my mouth and pulled my lips to his, crushing me in a passionate kiss. I thrust my hips into him, riding his erection through the denim of his jeans.

"Babe, you're going to be late," he groaned as he slid both hands into the back of my jeans and panties and palmed the cheeks of my ass roughly.

"I can make time," I whispered before nipping at the lobe of his ear.

"Fuck."

"Mmm," I hummed at his ear. I loved when he lost control during sex and the dirty words started falling from his mouth. I kissed his lips before standing and peeling my jeans down my thighs, my panties falling to the ground with them. He worked the zipper down on his pants and pulled his cock out in his hands. My heart skipped a few beats and another wave of pleasure rushed between my thighs. I crawled back on top of him and pressed myself against his length, sliding it back and forth between my swollen lips.

"Christ, Georgia. I can't fucking wait anymore."

"Patience brings sweet rewards." I worked myself over him, the head of his cock hitting my clit and sending sparks of lust through my body.

"You're a vixen. The devil in disguise," he groaned as his hips worked in deliciously slow circles. He passed across my entrance and tried to thrust into me, but I lifted my hips out of his reach. "Jesus, baby," he growled before throwing his head against the chair, exposing his throat to me. I lowered back down and continued to tease, not letting him inside me as my hands worked their way up his beautiful throat, the stubble along his jaw, and entwined in his hair. My lips kissed along the cords of his neck and over his Adam's apple. I licked and flicked my tongue along the sharp lines of his jaw, enjoying his taste.

"You're so beautiful," I breathed into his ear as my teeth scraped along the shell of it.

"You're such a tease." His hands held my hips firmly in place as he tried to angle himself into me.

"I take pleasure in watching you come undone," I murmured.

"Sadist." His fingers dug into my ass as he tried to impale himself on me. I lifted and then teased the head of his cock at my entrance. "Jesus, Georgia. I'm going to fucking come before I'm even inside you."

"Sounds like you should see a doctor about that," I murmured before his hand swiftly came down on my ass, causing a sting and, I'm sure, leaving a fiery handprint.

"Ow. Fuck."

His eyes held mine, blazing with lust before he thrust into me, hard and fast and unforgiving. A groan passed my lips as my head arched in pleasure. "Fuck, that's a beautiful face. The way you look when I'm buried inside you." He thrust up into me as I rode him in his office chair. His hands held my hips firmly as he worked himself in and out of me. "I need you deeper, baby." He lifted me, his dick still buried between my thighs, and laid me out across his desk. He pushed paperwork to one side and pounded between my thighs, working in and out of me, his beautiful face tense with pleasure.

"This is us, right here. You and me and no one else. Just this." His hand circled around my clit and I could feel another orgasm building. The small bud swelled and burned with release. "You like when I'm buried inside you, baby? When I fuck you over my desk?"

"God, yes," I whimpered as he thrust into me at a punishing pace. My hands flew to my breasts and I kneaded and pinched at the nipples, causing fire to race through my body. "I'm going to come."

"Wait. Wait for me beautiful," he ground through a clenched jaw. I reached a hand between us and wrapped my fingers around the base of him where our bodies met as he pounded in and out of me. "Jesus, baby." His thrusts sped up, his eyes trained on mine, lust pouring off him, causing my skin to tingle and prickle. "Georgia." He said my name and my body shuddered around him, coming undone for him because only he did this to me. Only ever him. He knew my body—could read it as well as his own—and had me convulsing in pleasure around his cock as he pounded into me, seeking his own release, before his hands clenched into my flesh and his body shuddered against mine.

He throbbed as my body milked every ounce he had to

give. His eyes fluttered closed and his head fell down on my chest. Golden hair tickled my breasts as gasps wracked his body. I held him tight to me, so tight I could never let him go. He gave me everything he had each time we were together, and I felt it. He was always with me. It was unlike anything I'd ever experienced before.

I lifted my hand, the weight of the ring he'd given me alerting me to its presence. The diamond glittered in the sunlight and tears pricked beneath my eyelids. I was so happy. So full when we were together. I wanted for absolutely nothing as long as he was in my arms.

I weaved my fingers into his sexy bed-head hair and held onto him for dear life. If he ever left, it would destroy me. There was no one else for me but him, and after all I'd gone through with Kyle, I was only sad it'd taken me so long to see it. Tristan and I had gone through hell and back together, and my body calmed at the notion we would only get better. Things could only go up for us.

"I love you so fucking much," Tristan murmured as his hands skimmed up either side of my torso, his elbows propped on the desk beside me. He lifted his upper body off me and looked in my eyes. "I made you late," he murmured against my lips.

"No better reason to be late than having a fuck on your desk." A smile tipped my lips.

"Jesus, Georgia." He nipped at my lips, a beautiful grin breaking out across his face. "I want to keep you here all day. Chain you to my desk and make you my sex slave." He arched a flirty eyebrow.

"Didn't know you were so kinky." I grinned and clenched my core around him.

He sucked in a sharp breath as he slowly began to pull out of me. The slow drag of his cock against my hypersensitive nerves made a small moan escape my throat. "I can do kinky, baby. I can do whatever you need me to do as long as I get to bury myself between your beautiful thighs." He flashed me a heart-stopping grin.

I locked my legs around his waist before he could fully pull out of me. "Not yet," I murmured and pulled him back to me. I wrapped my arms around his sweat-slicked body and traced my nails up and down his back. A shiver ran through him as he tucked his nose beneath my ear and ran one hand into my messy hair.

"You're going to be late," he muttered.

"I want to stay here with you," I whispered into his hair, his intoxicating fresh scent taking over my senses.

"You've been waiting for this appointment for a long time." He traced a thumb over my eyebrow, across my lips, over my cheekbone.

"I don't want to go." I pouted.

"I don't want you to go either, but you have to, baby," he whispered as he slowly pulled out of me. I shut my eyes tight and held my breath, enjoying the last sensations that ran through me as he pulled out. I sucked my lip between my teeth and shut my eyes tight. He was still hard. Jesus, I couldn't get enough of him.

"Baby, don't make that face," he muttered once he was disconnected from me.

"What?" My eyes flashed open in confusion.

"Like you want me again."

"I do."

"You're a horny girl. Insatiable," he muttered before kissing my lips and then pulling away to tuck himself back into his jeans. My lips turned down in a pout.

"Up and at 'em." He slapped my bare thigh playfully.

"I just want to stay here." I stretched my arms up over my head, feeling my muscles pulling taut. A groan escaped Tristan's throat before I looked up at him. His eyes darted across my body, landing on my pebbled nipples.

"So fucking hot." He skimmed a hand up my stomach and between my breasts. My nerves reawakened and my nipples hardened painfully. "Oh no, you have to go." He gave my nipple a rough pinch before picking up my jeans and panties and tossing them in my direction. My eyes clouded with lust as he turned to pick up the paperwork from the floor that had fallen when he'd thrown me on the desk.

"Insatiable." He shook his head when he caught the look in my eyes. I grinned before peeling myself off his desk and pulling my panties and jeans up my thighs.

"Do I look thoroughly fucked?" I grinned.

"You've got a potty mouth, Miss Montgomery." He wrapped a hand into my hair and kissed my lips. "Now get to your appointment." He swatted me on the ass before I turned. I gave my hips a seductive shake and threw him a grin over my shoulder, leaving his office and heading to my first therapy appointment.

Twenty-Five

Tristan

At the end of May, we got a call that had us rushing down to Jacksonville. Drew was in labor, more than a week late, and Georgia wasn't willing to miss it for the world. She'd hired a caretaker for the house and a maid to come in, between guests. I'd come to realize it might be difficult for her to live right next door and I wondered if buying the tiny beach cottage next to the beach rental had been a good idea. It seemed to add an extra layer of stress, but so far, whenever I mentioned moving or buying something else, she wouldn't hear of it. I hoped that the stress would ease with time and, other than taking care of the big things, she could put the rental out of her mind.

We took the Jeep down to Jacksonville, Charlie in the back, and stayed for a week after little Bennett was welcomed into the world. Georgia attended labor and delivery with Drew and Gavin. Drew, through a haze of blissful tears, asked Georgia to be the little guy's godmother. She happily accepted. Regardless of the title, I knew she would be like a second mom to him. She had presents stacked in the back of the Jeep on the drive down, bought more when we were there, and helped out with feedings and diaper changes all through the night.

When we left a week later, the sad look on Georgia's face nearly broke my heart. She was leaving a piece of her heart with that squirmy little shit and it softened my heart to her and our future together all the more.

Another month passed, and we were in full summer swing. The beach house was booked through September and we were getting off-season calls for October. Turned out owning a rental on the North Carolina beach was a great investment, one that would more than pay the bills with little effort. All it took was some upkeep in between rentals, which we, for the most part, hired out when needed. Georgia had started writing in her free time; her new therapist had explained it was a form of therapy. A way to release the pain and fear she'd held onto for so long. She enjoyed it, and I loved watching her in the morning on the deck, laptop across her legs as she typed away. I didn't know what she was writing down and I didn't ask. I just knew that a sense of calm seemed to radiate out from her when she finally put it down for the day.

Georgia also received a letter from the parole board stating parole had been denied. I held her in my arms as she sobbed; her reaction surprised me at first. Wasn't this what she wanted? What she hoped for? Until she explained it was a cleansing of sorts. Happy tears and sad tears together: happy because she didn't want him released after serving just sixteen years for the brutal murder of her parents, but also sadness because he had a family he'd left abandoned—a wife without her husband and a son without a father. I didn't agree with this line of thinking at all; for all we knew, they were much better off without him, but I kept my mouth shut and let her cry. It was the least I could do.

We were also starting to talk about wedding plans. I was on her ass to set a date. I wasn't willing to let her slip through my fingers or give her a chance to wise up and dump my ass. I knew I had it good; I knew with my past, she could easily choose to be wary. She was old hat at relationships but I was a newbie. The old me would have been scared. The notions of a family and wife were new to me—something I hadn't given much thought to before—but now it was here, I wasn't worried in the slightest.

I was pushing for a fall wedding, but Georgia rolled her eyes every time I tried to convince her. She wanted something well-thought-out and planned. She argued she'd moved in with me on impulse and said yes on impulse, but she was not willing to get married on impulse. After weeks of working on her, I finally got her nailed down for spring. She wanted a small wedding on the beach, right here at our home, just our closest friends and family. It sounded perfect.

We were having this very discussion on a warm day at the beginning of July when a loud knock sounded at the door. Georgia lifted her eyebrows in surprise and then slid back through the French doors. She called my name a few minutes later, so I tracked in after her. I stepped up behind her, sliding my palm up her neck and giving her a soft massage before my eyes turned to the guest standing at the doorway.

"What's up?" I asked my beautiful fiancée, who was looking up at me with a confused expression.

"Tristan?" The woman in the doorway murmured my name. I glanced at her, searching her face. I was sure I didn't know her. "It's okay, baby." She pulled a little boy, not more than three or four, from behind her. A mass of tousled blond hair and light green eyes stared back at me. "This is your daddy, honey."

My heart roared in my ears. It beat so fucking fast I swore it would fly out of my chest. I met the woman's eyes, unable to speak, searching for answers. I didn't fucking know her. At least I didn't think I knew her. But that kid—that kid could have been me at four. His hair, his eyes, I didn't want to believe it, but the resemblance couldn't be denied.

"I'll let you guys talk." Georgia pulled away from me.

"No. Don't leave." I pulled her closer to me, searching her eyes, begging her not to walk away. I swallowed the huge lump that had formed in my throat. I felt Georgia shuffle beside me. Shit, I'd forgotten how she must be feeling. She must have been able to see how much he looked like me. Would she run? Would this be the last straw? This summer had been so perfect, everything about it—from our engagement on—and was it all about to shatter at my feet?

The sad thing was I couldn't blame her if she did run.

This was her greatest fear. Her biggest insecurity when it came to us—my past. And here it was, three feet tall and starting up at me.

"It's okay." I watched her take a deep breath. "Hey, little guy, want to take a walk with me? We can look for sea glass on the shore." She bent down to his level and I watched their interaction, tears burning the back of my eyes. I ran a hand through my hair and pulled. I was going to be fucking bald before I hit thirty, without a doubt. I chomped down on my lip painfully. I couldn't imagine what Georgia was feeling, but if this kid was mine, I had to be there. It just tore me up inside that I couldn't have this with Georgia, because she was the girl I wanted. I didn't want this with anyone but her, but now here we were, another wrench thrown in our path.

"What's sea glass?" his soft little voice asked her.

"Here, lemme show you."

His little hand slipped into hers. His mom nodded to Georgia in agreement before the girl who stole my heart, and the little person that may or may not have my DNA coursing through his little body, turned the corner and walked out toward the beach.

"Are you sure? I mean, I don't really remember . . ."

"I'm not surprised you don't remember. We hooked up one night in Jacksonville more than four years ago and that little guy was the result."

"No fucking way." I shook my head in disbelief. But it couldn't be denied. He looked just fucking like me. I was sure I could dig up a baby picture that had me looking just like him. "Impossible." I stared at her, unable to rip my gaze away.

"I'm sorry it took me so long. I didn't have your number, and the situation being what it was . . . I just didn't think you'd want . . ." She trailed off.

"Yeah." I shuffled to the side and invited her in. We had four years worth of talking to do but I couldn't calm down; my heart thudded and my breath came out in quick exhales.

I can't fucking breathe. Jesus Christ, is it hot in here?

My brain buzzed with a million thoughts, all the time my eyes searching her face.

Blue eyes. High cheekbones. Long legs. Light blonde hair.

Why didn't I know her? Why didn't she look familiar? I'd been with a lot of women, but fuck—I never thought I'd forget a face like this.

Twenty-Six

Georgia

I walked down to the water with a little fist clenched in my hand. The sweetest little boy I'd ever laid eyes on—a little boy who could easily be Tristan's son. I tried to distract myself with small talk as we picked our way along the shoreline, pointing out shells, watching the sea birds, throwing sticks for Charlie to fetch, as his mom and possibly his dad talked in my house.

Our house.

The kitchen we made dinners in.

The bedroom we made love in.

The living room we planned our wedding in.

The house I'd been envisioning our kids growing up in, and yet here was this little guy, a product of Tristan's one-night stand with someone else. The thought wrenched my heart into two painful, jagged pieces.

"What's your name, sweetheart?" I bent beside him as

he drew swirls in the sand with his finger.

"Trevor," he said in a singsong voice. "You're pretty."

"Thanks, Trevor." God, even his name was close to Tristan's. She'd named him after his dad.

Tristan and Trevor. My heart galloped inside my chest cavity, beating against the walls and threatening to burst out.

I suddenly felt lightheaded and plopped my ass in the wet sand.

The worst part was she seemed perfectly nice. She didn't seem vindictive. I'd run into a few of Tristan's exes and he had a type. Bleached blonde and bitchy, and while she was blonde, she didn't seem at all bitchy. Other than the fact that she'd announced to this little boy that Tristan was his dad before she'd even spoken to Tristan about it, she seemed perfectly honest. Understanding.

I was about to throw up.

I took deep breaths and watched the little boy's wavy golden locks fall over his forehead as he drew stick figures.

Jesus, he looked like one of the little kids I'd imagined in my daydream last summer. Except this one wasn't mine. He was Tristan's and this beautiful little boy's mother's. Another woman. The product of another night of passion Tristan had had with someone other than me. It didn't matter we hadn't known each other then; he'd always been mine.

We'd belonged to each other, were meant to find each other from the beginning, and it felt like such a loss of a dream, having kids together, because now he might have a child with someone else.

And then I remembered we didn't know for sure.

But God, he looked so much like him: the odds were in favor of Tristan being this beautiful little boy's daddy. I ran a hand through my hair, a habit I was picking up from Tristan, and took a few deep, calming breaths.

I didn't know what it would mean for us if this was his child. I didn't know if I could stay. I loved him, but this was so much. Custody and visitation and shared vacations. My mind ran away with all the potential complications this could hold for our future.

Could this break us?

I knew I loved Tristan. I knew this little boy deserved his daddy. I just didn't know if I could be a stepmom. I didn't know if I could look into the face of this little boy who looked so much like Tristan: a reminder of a shared night he'd had with another woman.

I didn't know if I had it in me.

I walked into our bedroom and found Tristan propped

against the headboard, staring off into space. I frowned at his vacant expression. His mind was consumed with thoughts; I could see them running a thousand miles a minute. I tried to quell the anxiety that had been building in my tummy all day. Tristan and Lexi had spent two hours talking at the kitchen table while Trevor and I played on the beach with Charlie, making sand castles and splashing in the waves. He'd asked me if Tristan was really his daddy. He'd said that he'd never had a daddy before. I told him I didn't know, but with every word he said, my heart broke for him.

I took my time going through my evening routine of brushing my teeth and washing my face, because I was dreading crawling into bed with Tristan. After Lexi and Trevor left, Tristan had locked himself in his office. I didn't know what he was doing, or thinking, but I didn't bother him. I knew he needed just as much time to adjust to this as I did.

"Hey." I crawled into bed beside him. He snapped out of his thoughts and curled an arm around my shoulder, tucking me into his body. He dipped down and kissed the top of my head, nuzzling his nose in my hair. I squeezed my eyes shut tight and melted into him. I burrowed into his chest and enjoyed the feeling of his soft skin against mine. I swallowed down the lump in my throat, but wasn't able to calm the raging of my heart.

"I have to take care of him." Tristan murmured into my hair. "He looks . . . he looks so much . . ." He sucked in a quick breath and held it, like he was waiting for my reaction.

"I know," I whispered. Trevor looked just like him. Chances were good that Tristan was his dad. Tristan's fingers kneaded into the muscle of my neck and I could tell he was staring into space again, his thoughts taking him away.

"Lexi and Trevor are in town for a few days. I asked her if I could take him out, spend some time with him." Tristan stood across the kitchen from me the next morning, coffee cup in hand, hip resting against the counter and sexy as ever.

"Okay." I stood and watched him, waiting for more, but unable to ask the questions, unwilling to pry.

"You don't mind?"

"No." I obsessively wiped the countertop down with a towel, anything to avoid looking in his eyes.

"Are you sure? I just don't want to miss anymore time with him."

"How long will she be in town?" That question came out clipped. I didn't mean it to, but it rolled out before I'd had a chance to catch it.

"She took a few weeks off. Once she tracked me down, she figured we'd need time to figure things out . . ."

"Do you remember her?" I asked without looking up at him. He didn't answer right away, the waves rolling on the shore becoming louder and louder with each passing moment of silence that stretched between us.

"I'm not sure."

I finally peeked up at him as he ran a hand through his hair.

"Did she tell you anything about . . . that night?" The words barely escaped my throat. It physically hurt to say them.

"She said we were at a little sports bar. A place I used to go to a lot. She said we took shots and played pool, and I was pretty wasted by the end of the night. She drove me home; she said it seemed like I was going through something."

"What do you mean?"

"Like I was looking to forget something. Or someone," he mumbled and looked away from me.

"Oh. Do you think . . ." I trailed off.

"She's telling the truth?" His eyes darted back to mine.

"I don't know. I don't see why she wouldn't. She knew where I lived . . ." He gnawed on his bottom lip once he'd finished. "Four and a half years ago—the month it would have happened—would have been my birthday."

"Oh." My brows knit together in confusion.

"And the anniversary of my mom leaving," he said so softly I had to strain to hear him.

"What?" I whispered.

"My mom left on my birthday. We had a birthday party, cake, pictures, everything was perfect, and then late that night . . . she left. Every birthday was hard for me—the anniversary of her leaving. I always got shitfaced to forget. So when she says it seemed like I was going through something . . . I was."

My thoughts slammed through my head. Oh God, Trevor was his son. He'd had a one-night stand with Lexi. One night and they'd made a baby.

"Well, I've got stuff to do, so . . . I'll see you in a few hours?"

"Georgia." He set down his coffee cup and made his way toward me.

"No, it's okay. Just go be with Trevor. He's sweet; enjoy him."

"Do you want to come?" Tristan's eyes lit up.

"No, I can't. I really have stuff I need to take care of.

Calls and . . . whatever. So I'll see you later?" I turned to leave the kitchen.

"Georgia, wait."

I turned and watched him watching me. His eyes held a look of pain and confusion and anxiety. His shoulders were hunched over, both hands shoved in the pockets of his worn jeans. His white shirt fitted to his lean form. I wanted to run to him, press my nose into the fresh cotton, and inhale him. Take a hit of my favorite scent in the world, one that helped to center me.

"I'm afraid you won't be here when I get back." His eyes peered back at me. The pain that radiated across the kitchen held me stock-still, gazing back at him. I swallowed the lump that had lodged in my throat.

"I'll be here." I stepped up to him, running a hand along his cheek, feeling the stubble along his jaw line. "I'll be here," I murmured. His green eyes assessed me with a vulnerability I'd never seen before. It terrified me and broke my heart all in the same breath. I had the ability to destroy him if I left, and I'd never felt that before. He'd said that months ago and I'd believed him, but now I was seeing the concern etched across his face.

He didn't trust me not to leave.

"I love you." He snagged my hand, pulled my wrist up to his lips, and placed a soft kiss on my skin. "Every day, I love you." He turned my hand over and placed a kiss on the glittering diamond I wore on my ring finger.

"I know." I nodded and leaned into him. He enveloped me in his arms and rubbed my back. "I love you too," I choked out as tears finally fell down my cheeks. I held him against me, letting the worry and anxiety seep out of my system. I was so ready for our path to be steady and straight, not rocky, with bumps in the road and obstacles meant to throw us off. I didn't know how much more we could take.

We stood there for an untold amount of minutes, holding each other, taking comfort because neither of us knew the path that lay ahead.

Twenty-Seven

Tristan

I stepped out onto the deck a few mornings later to find Georgia in the sweetest little short fucking cut-offs, her creamy skin revealed nearly up to there, so indecent all I could think about was twisting one fist in her wild fucking hair and running the other up her leg until I reached her pussy. Tingles raced across the base of my spine and my dick twitched in my shorts. I would never get enough of her; she had my blood set to a constant boil, ready to take her, make her mine at any given moment, regardless if I'd just been buried deep inside her.

She stood on the beach barefoot, her hair dancing on the wind, staring into the distance. With coffee cup in hand, I headed down the steps, ready to make my way to her when she turned a fraction and I saw the phone at her ear. Who could she possibly be talking to this early? I frowned and glanced at my watch. Before nine a.m.

I stood, content to watch her beautiful form on the beach, waiting for her to get off the phone. Charlie sauntered around in the sand, dipping his big paws into the water and sniffing around the dune grass. This was my life and it was beyond fucking perfect. My beautiful dark-haired girl had made my life perfect, and the guilt I felt for throwing her into my mess burned in my stomach. I'd thrown her such a load of shit lately. I cast my eyes down to the sand, watching the wind scatter it across the weathered wood of the deck.

If Trevor was mine, I had to be there for him. I had to be a dad, there wasn't any other option. I just prayed with everything I had in me that Georgia wouldn't leave me.

But who could blame her if she did?

I hadn't known she would come. That a beautiful dark-haired woman would consume me, make me drop to my knees, make me want to give up everything I thought I wanted just for a taste, a glimpse of her smile, a touch of her skin. If she left me, I'd be torn apart. I'd have my son, but I'd be a hollow fucking shell and my heart would cease to beat. I took a long swallow of my coffee and tried to shift my focus away from what-ifs. There was nothing I could do anyway. I didn't have any other options ahead of me.

Finally, she turned and caught my eyes. Her brows furrowed for a moment and her bottom lip snagged between her teeth before she glanced away. Odd reaction to seeing me. I knew we were going through some stuff and we hadn't really spoken about Trevor and Lexi, but she looked like she was trying to hide something, which wasn't at all like her. I waited for her on the deck, sipping my coffee, my brain running wild with the possibilities of who she could be talking to.

Finally, she turned back to me and shoved the phone in her pocket. She took slow steps and when she finally reached me, I sat my coffee cup on the railing and pulled her into my arms.

"Hey, there," I mumbled, my lips pressed into the soft hair on the top of her head.

"Hey." She locked her hands around my waist.

"On the phone so early?" I fingered the silky strands of her hair between my fingers.

"Mhmm." She nuzzled her nose into my neck and I heard her inhale deeply. She took comfort from my scent as much as I did hers. I could feel it. She always tucked her nose in my neck and inhaled. The day she stopped doing that, I would worry. It brought me comfort after the way my mind had run away with me a few minutes ago. The truth was, I was terrified she'd run back to her first love, even if he hadn't treated her well.

"Who was it?" I muttered as fear clenched my heart,

suddenly afraid it had been Kyle.

"No one." She held me tighter to her lean body.

"No one so early in the morning?"

"No one that matters," she mumbled and dipped her fingertips inside the waistband of my jeans.

"Stop trying to distract me." I grinned, thrusting my hips into her so she could see just how distracted I was.

"You don't need my help with that; he's got a mind of his own." She leaned back and a beautiful grin split across her face.

"You're so fucking beautiful in the morning." I ducked my head and caught her lips with mine. I pulled away and stroked her eyebrow with the pad of my thumb. "You'd tell me if things weren't okay, right?"

"Of course." She pulled away from me.

"Because despite everything, I . . . I'm afraid . . ."

"Afraid of what?" Her beautiful browns were locked on my own. I was suddenly uncomfortable and squirming.

"I'm just afraid that everything with Trevor and Lexi, it could be too much," I finished as I diverted my gaze over her head and out to the frothing waves at the shore. Charlie had found a stick and was chewing it between both his paws. I made a mental note to ask the vet about splinters in his gut or intestines or some shit. That couldn't be good for anybody.

“I would tell you if it was.”

“Okay.” I wrapped my arms around her body and held her tightly to me, too afraid to let her go at this moment. I needed to feel her. Needed her scent to surround me, to comfort me.

“Babe, it’s that unknown number again.” I ignored the call on Georgia’s phone and the recent calls list popped up. I frowned as I looked at all the times the unknown number had called. My eyes zeroed in on the call she’d taken this morning when I’d been watching her on the beach.

Unknown.

She’d been talking to whoever it was. I scrolled through quickly and saw that the only time she’d spoken to the caller was this morning. That gave me some relief. I pulled my bottom lip between my teeth and looked up from her phone, wanting to snoop, feeling like a douche for wanting to snoop, but she’d been evasive with me this morning, and after all the upheaval lately . . .

I went to her recent text messages and found her phone blasted with messages from the unknown number.

“What the fuck?” I mumbled as I flipped through them quickly.

Talk to me.

Pick up.

I need to talk to you.

I'm sorry.

I miss you.

What. The. Fuck.

It had to be Kyle. I knew it with every hyper-alert nerve in my body. He'd been blowing up her phone for weeks now and she'd finally answered him this morning, just a few days after Lexi had shown up on my doorstep. This wasn't fucking good. Not fucking good at all. My heart leaped into my throat. I slammed her phone down on the kitchen counter and ran a hand over my face and through my hair. I gave an angry tug as I debated what to do.

It wasn't my business to be scrolling through her phone, but why the fuck had she lied? Was she still seeing him? Was she leaving me for him? Had more happened than she'd let on back in DC? I knew I had to be smart, play this stealth, beat around the bush, look for clues, but my anger surged and I knew I didn't have the patience to be smart about anything in that moment.

In the past, with any other fucking girl, I would have cut my losses and walked away. In fact, I wouldn't have allowed any other girl to get this close at all and this was exactly the reason why.

Jesus Christ, everything my dad said had been true. True love is fleeting. Women bore easily and leave quickly.

"Fuck," I growled as I slammed my palm on the countertop again.

"What's wrong?" Her singsong voice, the one that had my heart skipping beats, floated through the room as she walked in the kitchen, fresh from the shower. She was towel drying her wet ringlets, wearing a thin tank top, obviously without a bra. Wetness from her hair dampened the fabric and made the outline of her perfect pink nipples stand out. She wore a pair of baby pink lace trimmed underwear and that was it. A growl escaped my throat as my eyes darted up her body. A crooked smile lit her lips and lust burned in her eyes once she realized where my thoughts had gone. She arched a playful eyebrow and licked her lips seductively.

"Something got your attention?" she breathed as she stepped closer. I clenched my eyes shut tightly, her citrus soap invading my senses. Fuck, I wanted to grill her for answers and plow into her, make her mine, mark her all in the same instant.

"Who the fuck were you talking to this morning?" I whispered, anger vibrating off my body. She sucked in a sharp breath and I opened my eyes. Her gorgeous browns flickered down to the counter to her phone. Suddenly, tension filled her frame and her spine straightened. She held the towel in one hand, crossing her arms defensively. Her defensive stance would have worked too, if it wouldn't have pushed her tits together, the fabric tightening across her nipples and making my semi-hard cock rise to full attention.

"Clearly you've got an issue, so why don't you tell me who you think it was?"

"Kyle." I ground the word out, hatred more than clear in my voice. She narrowed her eyes at me, but refused to answer. "Was it that fucking prick?"

Her head tipped to the side, wet ringlets falling over her shoulder, her chocolate eyes blazing with anger. "Yes."

"What the fuck, Georgia?"

"What?"

"What do you mean *what*? Why didn't you tell me he's the one that's been blowing up your phone, who you were talking to this morning?"

"I said it was no one that mattered. That's true." An angry flush had settled high on her cheekbones. The same rosy shade that colored her breasts when she was aroused.

"I had a right to know he's been calling you. And fucking texting."

"How do you know he's been texting? Did you look through my phone, Tristan?" She tipped her head to one side, trying to catch me in a lie.

"Yep. I was suspicious after all these unknown calls and

turns out I had a right to be."

"Of course you didn't. I haven't even talked to him before this morning."

"Did more happen when you went back to DC? More you didn't tell me?"

"You mean more than lunch and the introduction to his baby mama? No," she spat. Georgia was fiery when she was angry, and she was also beautiful and sexy and hot as hell, and I could feel my anger evaporating, being replaced by something else, something stronger.

Lust.

The need to have her body. All of it. Because the thought had slammed into my brain, rattling me from the sense of comfort I'd felt, just because I'd put a ring on her finger didn't mean she wouldn't leave.

Looking at her now, standing across from me, it hit me like a ton of bricks that she could just as easily slip that ring off her finger and walk away from me. After all, she'd done it to Kyle.

I swallowed and tried to control the emotions boiling in me. I was pretty sure my advances wouldn't be welcome at this moment when the rage was rolling off her—after I'd just accused her of lying and cheating.

"Uh uh. Oh no." She backed away a few steps.

"What?" I pitched my head to the side.

"I know that look. I'm pissed at you, mister."

"What look?" The slightest smile tugged at my lips.

"That look like you want to devour me."

"How astute. That's exactly what I want to do." I took two long strides to her and wrapped a hand around her neck, crashing her lips to mine, owning her, tasting her, devouring her. Doing exactly what I'd been fighting the last few minutes. I tugged the top of her tank top down to reveal her bare breasts, plucked a budded pink nipple between my fingers as she twisted and moaned into my mouth. Her hands wrapped my hair and her hips pressed against my own. I bent her back over the kitchen table, her body lying out before me as my lips attached to that beautiful pink bud. I sucked and pulled and tugged, causing her to writhe with pleasure.

"I'm still mad at you," she moaned as I thumbed her other nipple.

"Is that why your pussy is dripping wet?" I shifted the fabric of her panties aside and dragged two fingers up her wet and swollen lips. She arched and groaned before I thrust two fingers inside her. "This is mine," I muttered before dragging my teeth across her hardened pink nipple. I kneaded her breast with one hand, pressing and palming, digging my fingers into her soft flesh. She panted and wiggled, thrusting her hips up into my hand, riding my fingers to her orgasm.

"This," I hooked my fingers inside her and pulled against the swollen spot deep inside her body, "is just for me." I tore the scrap of lace off her body and attached my lips to her throbbing clit. "Only I taste this. Only I'm inside this beautiful tight pussy. You only scream my name." I sucked and dragged my fingers along her throbbing walls before she came undone all around my hand. The heat seeped out of her as she panted and moaned my name, one hand fisted in her hair, her lean body arched off the table, tits thrust high in the air.

Before giving her a chance to recover, I unbuckled my belt and popped the button on my jeans, pulling them down my thighs before I slammed my aching cock into her soft body. I pumped ruthlessly, taking her, pummeling my anger into every thrust.

"You own my fucking heart, Georgia, and I own this." I smoothed one palm up the center of her stomach, between her breasts, my hand wrapped around her delicate neck, the pad of my thumb caressing her pulse point. "He had you once, and he fucked it up. I would never." I thrust into her, circling my hips to hit her higher. "I would never fucking do to you what he did." I dug my fingers into the creamy flesh of her thigh and hiked it around my waist. "Do you hear me?" I leaned over her body, my lips attaching to her neck, kissing and suckling. "I would never hurt you. And if you left . . ." My thrusts eased into a steady rhythm. My release burned low at my spine, my balls reaching an unbearable tingle. I was so fucking close to losing it, but it didn't matter, because I'd already lost everything to her. She'd taken it, taken me completely. "If you left, it would shatter me. I wouldn't survive it," I murmured softly as my orgasm tore through my body, flooding my veins, from my legs straight out to my fingertips.

"I wouldn't survive you, Georgia," I murmured as I dropped her thigh from my waist and ran both of my fingers into her damp hair. I pulled her mouth to mine and caressed her with my lips, our tongues tangling together, dancing and caressing, smoothing and tasting.

"I love you, Tristan. And I would never . . ." she murmured before I cut her off with another desperate kiss. Her mouth took mine before she pulled away and finished, her lips dusting against my own. "I won't leave you."

I nodded and tucked my head into the crook of her shoulder. Her palms smoothed over my back, nails dragging against the cotton of my shirt and through to my skin. Every fucking moment, this girl awed me. My beautiful dark-haired beauty. And yet each time it happened, I was still shocked at the depths she owned me.

"Do you want to talk about it?"

We lay curled up on the couch, a blanket thrown over our still naked bodies.

"Mmm," I murmured, my arm wrapped around her torso, holding her tight to me. My tongue darted out and tasted the flesh along her neck.

"Is that a yes?" She giggled.

"That's an 'I don't care as long as my tongue is on your body.'"

"I like that one too," she whispered. "But I want to tell you. I thought about telling you, but I just needed a minute to process . . ." She turned in my arms, her hand cupping my cheek.

I pouted at the loss of contact. "'Kay, go for it, sweetheart."

"It was Kyle," she started before I narrowed my eyes and groaned. I hated his fucking name rolling off her lips. "But . . ." She gave me a light tap on the cheek with a grin. "He just wanted to apologize, for everything, I guess. She's having the baby soon." When she said that, her eyes drifted off into space. I frowned; I knew she didn't want his baby *per se*, but just the idea of him having a baby at all brought sadness to her eyes. At one time that was supposed to be her. I pushed that thought from my mind because if there was anyone's baby she'd carry inside her body, it would be mine.

"He wanted to know how I was. If we were okay. If you treated me well." She looked back at me, a soft smile lighting her full lips. I rolled my eyes. Too little too fucking late, buddy.

"What'd you tell him?"

"That you make me come so hard I forget my own name."

I started coughing and my eyes bugged out as I took in the grin that had crossed her face.

"You smart ass." I smacked her on the bare flesh of her bottom.

"You love my smart ass." She wiggled underneath the blanket.

"It's a beautiful one," I murmured as I smoothed my palm across her round ass cheek and dusted my fingers along the sensitive flesh between her legs.

"Stop," she moaned.

"That stop sounded like a go." I dragged my fingers through the wetness, pleased to find she wanted me again.

"It was a stop," she finished breathlessly before grabbing my wrist and tugging it away from her ass. "Let me finish."

"Only if you promise to let me finish after you finish." I tugged at her nipple with my thumb and forefinger.

"You're a horny teenager. What did you do before me? Seriously? A blowup doll under the bed? Your hand?" she teased.

"No need for blowup dolls, baby," I grinned as her face fell. Fuck, I'd put my foot straight in my goddamned mouth. "I'm sorry," I offered as she turned away from me.

"It's okay. You've got a past. I knew that going in." She sucked in a sharp breath before continuing. "So he just wanted to apologize for all the cheating he'd done for all the years. Wanted to know that I was happy. He seemed . . . not happy. Remorseful, I guess," she said thoughtfully. "His baby is due next week, so I think he's just been thinking about a lot of stuff . . ." She trailed off, twirling a piece of the blanket between her fingers.

"Do you want a baby?" I tugged her chin up to look me in the eyes. She stared me down, her eyes searching my face, before landing back on my gaze.

"Yeah, of course."

"Soon?" My heart thudded in my chest. I wasn't sure what I wanted her answer to be, but for the first time in my life, it didn't terrify me. If she said yes, I would be okay with that.

"Maybe," she murmured, avoiding my gaze.

"Okay." It suddenly felt like a weight lifted off my shoulders. She wasn't going to leave me. If we were talking about having kids, she wasn't going to leave.

"Okay what?" She scrunched her eyebrows up in the most adorable way.

"Okay, we can talk about it when you're ready."

"Really? We're not even married." She rolled her eyes.

"Well, we will be sooner rather than later if I have anything to say about it." I pulled her chin to me and kissed her soft lips. "You're beautiful, and I already asked you to marry me. I want to be married. I want to have babies with you. Buckets full." My mouth curled into a lopsided grin.

"Buckets full of babies?" She giggled and my heart lifted a little more. If I could keep her smiling and happy, I would forever count my blessings.

"Buckets full of babies." I nodded and kissed her lips one last time. "But until then, I plan on practicing. A lot." I smacked her bare ass and she shrieked before darting off the couch and down the hallway. I jumped up and followed after her, because whether she knew it or not, I'd follow her. Whenever and wherever, I would always follow her.

Twenty-Eight

Tristan

"Hey, baby." I wrapped her in my arms when she curled up into my lap on the porch. She laid her head on my shoulder and inhaled deeply. She dusted her nose across my sensitive flesh; she was taking me in, scenting me, and it turned me on more than she could ever imagine. "Everything okay?" I tugged on her ponytail to make eye contact with her. Her brows were knit together, her eyes downcast as if she felt guilty about something. "I told you, I'm not mad about the Kyle thing." I rubbed my thumbs along her neck, easing her tense shoulders. It'd been a few days since the phone call she'd taken from Kyle and I was well past it. We were taking the obstacles on the road to our happily every after one bump at a time.

"It's not that," she said softly and then looked back to the frothing white waves rolling up the shore. I followed her gaze and watched Charlie trot along the shore.

"What is it?"

"I know this isn't my business and I know he may be your son, but what about a paternity test?" she mumbled so softly I had to strain to hear her. I watched her beautiful eyes glancing everywhere but at me. I could tell this was uncomfortable for her, and I loved her all the more for it.

I took in a deep breath of air, filling my lungs and then glancing back to Charlie. Diva sat by the screen door, a low meow escaping her throat. "She thinks she's part dog." The cat sat at the screen door and meowed all damn day until someone let her out.

Georgia glanced from her cat to me, a sad smile lighting her lips. She knew this was difficult for me.

"He looks just like me, Georgia."

"I know," she murmured before smoothing a hand across my cheek.

"It's just . . . I feel like the paternity test is insulting. It's like disowning him somehow. What if he is mine, and he finds out that I took a paternity test to prove it? Isn't that shitty? Like I didn't want him?"

"No, he doesn't have to find out . . . it's not like that . . . and he would know, in here." She pressed her palm to my chest, over my heart. "He would know you loved him, how much you love him." Her eyes searched mine. I could see she needed answers. I'd been avoiding this conversation, avoiding making this decision because of the guilt I carried over it. His mom and I had been irresponsible one night and he'd been the result and I hated knowing that. I hated the thought he would someday find out he'd been unintentional. I'd felt unwanted my entire fucking life, and here I was repeating the cycle, albeit in a different form.

"I know what you're thinking. I can see it in those big green eyes of yours." She stroked her thumb along my eyebrow, trying to soothe the pain away. "You'll love him if he's yours. He'll feel that every day. You just need to know."

"And you need to know?" I looked at her, not an ounce of judgment in my voice.

"We both do." Her eyes softened as her fingers continued to work on the skin behind my neck.

"What if he isn't?" I muttered, worrying the rim of the coffee cup with my fingertips.

"Then someone else needs to know he's his dad. He deserves the chance to be his dad. Just like you do if you are."

"Yeah," I mumbled thoughtfully.

"There's a place in Wilmington. Maybe you could go together and have the test done."

"They have to take his blood?" My eyes swung to hers with fear.

"No." She smiled. "Just a cheek swab. No blood." She kissed me full on the lips. I trailed my tongue along the seam, asking her to open to me. She did immediately, her lips pliable against mine. I wrapped my arm around her back and skimmed it up to her neck, holding her tightly, needing her to feel my love for her.

"Thank you." I pulled away, leaving one last kiss on the corner of her mouth.

"I'll set up an appointment, okay?"

"Okay." I caressed the skin of her shoulder as I gazed out at the water, lost in my thoughts.

"Is this test going to tell if you're my dad?" Trevor looked up at me, big innocent eyes trained on mine. My eyebrows arched up in surprise. Jesus, did Lexi tell him everything?

"Uhmm." I shot her a glare. She shrugged her shoulders.

"I had to tell him; he kept asking me why he needed a test when he wasn't sick."

"She told me they're testing my DMA."

"DNA, buddy, and, yeah, they are. Just to tell us some things." I ruffled his hair.

"Do you want to be my dad?" I opened the door of the clinic, my eyebrows shooting into my hairline.

"Yeah, of course. We have a lot of fun together, right?" I ran a hand through my hair. My heart galloped in my chest.

"Yeah, I told the kids at school how you took me to that baseball game and let me eat two hot dogs and nachos and have pop. Mom doesn't let me have pop."

"Shit, sorry," I mouthed to Lexi. A small smile lit her lips. She really was pretty, in an obvious sort of way. It was no wonder I was attracted to her, and motherhood looked good on her. She seemed to be good at it, more mature for it. Her long blonde hair was twisted into a side braid, jeans and a fitted top hugging her form. She bent down and whispered something in Trevor's ear. A frown danced across his face as he listened. I could see the resemblance between them. He may have had eyes that resembled mine, but the shape of his face and mouth were all her.

"I told him to stop asking so many questions."

"Mom said you're afraid of tests." Trevor looked up at me. "I'm not afraid of tests. Mom says to just take deep breaths and stay calm when I have one at school. Want me to teach you?"

A smile lit my lips at his innocence. "Sure, buddy." I placed a hand on his head and guided him to a chair in the waiting room while Lexi checked us in.

Fifteen minutes later, and we were walking back out the door. They'd swabbed our cheeks for DNA and now I was taking Trevor and Lexi to lunch. I'd left the decision up to Trevor where to go and he'd jumped on the chance at pizza, because apparently his mom didn't let him have that very often either.

We slid into a booth, Trevor next to me, and Lexi across the table. Before we could even order a pizza, I ordered a beer. I needed something to calm the thumping of my heart. Georgia had been right: at least now we would know, because not knowing was starting to kill me. Only thing was, I was growing attached to the little guy, so if he wasn't mine, that might kill me too.

Trevor rambled on about school and kids in his T-ball league as he picked the pepperoni off his pizza and ate all the cheese first before digging into the crust.

I was on my third beer when Lexi caught my attention. "Georgia's nice."

My eyes shot up in surprise. What was her game with this? Feeling me out? Seeing if I was ready to be a dad and a husband for her and Trevor? Because no fucking way, I was not signing up for that. If Trevor was mine I'd do everything I could for him but there was only one girl I wanted to tie myself to and it wasn't the blonde sitting in front of me. “Yeah,” I murmured and took another long draw of the amber liquid.

“It’s serious?”

“Serious enough to put a ring on her finger,” I muttered, unwilling to give her more information about Georgia. She was mine. That was between us. I wasn’t willing to let anyone else in our relationship.

“So the results will come to you, then?” She seemed to be making awkward conversation.

“That’s what they said, in thirty days or sooner.”

“Is she going to be all right if the test is positive?”

There it was. A snide comment. A snarky implication. “Are you trying to say something?” I angled my head to her.

“I just want to make sure she’s good for my son if she’s going to be in his life.”

My eyebrows shot up and I cleared my throat uncomfortably. “Georgia’s great with kids. She’ll be great.” I finished the rest of my beer and nodded the waiter over, signaling for the check. “Speaking of, I have to get back. Great seeing you, buddy. I’ll call you soon, okay? Be good for your mom.” I gave him a quick hug after he'd let me out of the booth.

“I’ll be in touch, Tristan,” Lexi called to my retreating form.

"I'm sure you will," I murmured to myself as I exited the restaurant and sucked in a gulp of fresh sea air. I needed to get home and back to my normal life. And I also needed some scotch. Beer just wasn't enough to get me through this day.

Twenty-Nine

Georgia

It'd been a month since Trevor and Lexi had knocked on our door. A month since Tristan had faced the possibility of being a dad. He'd spent as much time with Trevor as he could while they were here, taking him to museums and baseball games, and talked to him nearly every night on the phone. Tristan was determined to make it work: to be civil with Lexi, and to be the right kind of dad to Trevor, whom he was all but convinced was his.

I was so proud of him for taking responsibility and embracing his new role as someone's dad, but there was also a piece of me that hated my dream was shifting again. My dream to marry Tristan and have kids together was altering. We could do that, but now there was a little tousled-haired boy that was evidence of a night Tristan had shared with someone else.

Being separated and waiting on the paternity test results

was also starting to weigh in Tristan's eyes. Each night, we went to bed with an awkward silence, something unfamiliar between us.

I woke up on a Friday in August and knew I needed a break. I was sad that I needed a break from Tristan, but the truth was, he was currently in the midst of a lot of overwhelming, life-changing drama, and I needed time to process. I needed time to work through my thoughts without seeing his sad eyes peering back at me. I know he recognized the wall between us; it was just sad the wall was a beautiful little boy.

"Drew, come up. I need a girls' weekend," I moaned into the phone as soon as Drew picked up.

"Yeah?"

"The beach house is clear for the weekend. We'll camp out over there, just like last summer, the three of us. I need you guys," I nearly sobbed into the phone. Just the thought of a weekend with Drew and Silas had my emotions in overdrive. I needed my best friends. I needed them to help me forget and talk me through everything.

"Just the girls? No boys allowed?"

"Just Silas, I promise." I beamed because I knew she was caving.

"'Kay, let me see if Mom and Dad will take Bennett for the weekend and Gavin can have man-time with Tristan. All these diapers and breastfeeding are getting to him."

"Can't wait to see you."

"You too, honey." Drew hung up and I set the phone on the counter, wrapping a chenille blanket around my shoulders and propping my feet up on the deck as the cool early autumn air swept my hair around my face.

I'd only seen Drew once since Bennett had been born and I was looking forward to some time to escape the drama that had inserted itself into my life over the past month.

"Honey, I'm home," Drew's singsong voice echoed through the walls of the cottage. It felt like a repeat of last summer, except this time around, I was praying for less drama.

"Hey." I locked her in a tight embrace. "How are you, and how's my baby boy?"

"Everyone's good." She beamed. She looked so happy, blissfully so. Motherhood looked good on her. "In fact . . ." She held her left hand up and showed off a sparkling diamond the size of Texas.

"Jesus Christ, he could have fed a small country for the price of that." Silas stepped into the kitchen, margarita in hand.

"Shut up." Drew shot him a glare.

"Why the fuck do we need so much luggage to come for a weekend?" Gavin grunted as he let the bags fall from his shoulders. "We don't even have the kid with us. Hey, Georgia." He wrapped me in a one-armed hug.

"Hey, Daddy." I smiled up at him. "Finally making an honest woman out of my girl." I knocked my hip into hers playfully.

"She threatened bodily harm to my balls if I didn't." He grinned and winked at Drew.

"Shut up." She rolled her eyes before pecking him on the cheek.

"Where's my man?"

"Office." I nodded down the hallway.

"Don't get too comfortable; you have to haul my stuff over to Georgia's house," Drew called after him.

A snort sounded from down the hallway. It sounded like Gavin was in need of a guys' weekend just as much as I was a girls' weekend.

"Margarita, anyone?" Silas lifted the glass in his hand.

"Jesus, still an alcoholic, huh?" Drew knocked Silas in the arm.

"Hey, girls' weekend; I'm letting loose."

"I think you're loose enough as it is." Drew winked at me.

“Hey, married man, remember?” Silas lifted his hand and twisted the plain band on his ring finger.

“Right. Let’s get this weekend started.” She snatched Silas's drink and downed it in one guzzle.

“I thought you were breastfeeding?” I giggled at her.

“Oh, I am. I have to pump and dump.”

“Pump and what?” Silas's eyebrows knit together.

“After I drink I have to pump my breast milk and—”

“Okay, okay, TMI bitch. TMI.” Silas snatched his margaritas glass from her and turned to head out the door. Drew and I erupted into a fit of giggles.

“Babe! Bring my bags over to the beach house when you get a minute.”

Gavin huffed from down the hall and we all headed out the back door and made our way across the sand to the beach house. Silas poured us margaritas and we settled in for our weekend on the beach.

“So how’s it going, honey?” Drew curled her knees beneath her on the deck chair. We’d settled in with drinks and the three of us were perched on the deck, overlooking the rolling waves of the Atlantic.

“It’s going.” I sighed and sipped.

"Hardly," Silas grumbled.

"Yeah?" Drew's face turned down in sympathy.

It's hard." I shrugged.

"The baby-daddy situation is a bitch." Silas took another long draw of his drink.

"I would imagine. So what are you going to do about it?"

I heaved a sigh and swirled the slushy concoction in my glass.

What was I going to do about it? "I have no idea."

"Will you be supportive if he's Trevor's dad?" Drew's deep brown eyes searched my face.

"Yes . . . I think so . . ." I murmured as thoughts swirled in my head.

"What does that mean?"

"It means I want to be."

"She's trying to force it. Don't have guilt, love. This is your life, your decision. A little munchkin running around isn't exactly what you signed up for when you tapped that."

"Jesus, Silas." I laughed.

"He's right, G." Drew's eyes hit me with a serious glance. "So if he takes the test and he is the father," Drew announced in her best Maury Povich voice, "what are you going to do?"

I chewed on my bottom lip as I thought about the

possibility of Tristan being a dad. "I dunno." In all honesty, the thought shattered my heart.

"Will you stay?" Drew asked softly as tears began to pool in my eyes.

"I don't know that either." A tear fell down my cheek and I wiped it away forcefully. I didn't want to be weak. I wanted to roll with this. I wanted to be there for Tristan, no matter what.

I glanced down at the ring he'd given me and swirled it around on my finger. The beautiful diamond ring representing our love. Our life together. The vows we were soon supposed to take, in sickness and in health.

I knew that I should stand by him, but it was all so much to process. Was I being inflexible? Was I sticking to the course, the dreams I had for myself, unwilling to deviate? That's what had gotten me in trouble last summer. I thought that Kyle was my future, no matter what, even if our relationship had shifted to become less than ideal.

"I don't know if I can be with someone who is a father to someone else's kid." The words escaped my mouth as guilt suffocated me. Thoughts of that beautiful little blond-haired boy, the one that may have Tristan's blood surging through his veins, possessed my mind. His beautiful deep green eyes and heart-stopping smile. Could I turn my back on the man I loved because of one decision he'd made years ago?

I didn't want to. I desperately didn't want to, but the fact was, it was so much easier said than done.

"Let's face it; the kid is fucking cute. The real downer in this is bitchy-Barbie Lexi."

"Silas." I raised my voice before breaking out into laughter. The tequila was going to my head and it felt good. "It's so fucking true." I giggled before taking another sip.

"Enough of the baby-daddy drama. More drinks!" Silas lifted his glass, downed it, and then jogged back into the house to make more.

That night, I tossed and turned in my bed at the beach house. Silas, Drew, and I had moved down to the beach, toes dipped in the water as we sat and talked and laughed and drank. I'd gotten too drunk and the three of us finally stumbled to bed. A few minutes later, I'd heard heavy footsteps and Drew's bedroom door open and close. I knew she'd called Gavin to creep into her room—so much for girls' weekend. Apparently, it was girls' weekend until you were drunk and horny and wanted to slip between the sheets with your fiancé.

I heaved a sigh and turned up the music on my iPod,

trying to drown out the thoughts in my head and the creaking of the bed next door. I'd sobered up a little and real life drama had crept back in. I thrashed to the other side of the bed and buried my head in the pillow. My legs twitched and the covers twisted around my feet.

I missed him.

It felt so foreign to sleep by myself. I chewed on my bottom lip, as I thought about him in our house alone just a few yards away.

I pulled a pair of shorts up my legs and padded barefoot down the hallway and out the door. My feet hit the sand and I rushed across the beach to our house, the one Tristan and I shared together. My eyes took in the moonlight reflecting silvery sparkles off the midnight blue water. I dug my toes into the sand and inhaled the salty sweet air. I was going to get my man. The one I belonged with, regardless of his past; he was my future.

I made my way up the deck and slipped in the door. The house was silent and dark, moonlight reflecting off surfaces and shadows dancing in the corners. I made my way down the hall to our room. I slipped in through the door and stood, watching his lean form in bed. He lay on his stomach, sheet outlining his lean muscled back, elbows cocked to the side, forearms beneath the pillow at his head.

The moonlight glinted off the golden streaks in his

tousled hair and my fingers ached to tangle through it. I wanted to tuck my nose into his neck and inhale. I walked softly to the bed and crawled in next to him, running my hands up the smooth skin of his back. He rolled over, wrapped me in his arms, and held me tightly, never saying a word. I ran my nose along the line of his neck and took a hit of my favorite scent just below his ear. Butterflies danced in my stomach, and my heart swelled.

"I couldn't sleep without you," I whispered.

"I couldn't either." He nuzzled his nose into my hair and inhaled deeply. "I wanted to give you space if you needed it."

"I don't. I thought I did, but not from you. I only want to be right here," I murmured as he stroked my hair and held me tightly to him. I leaned up and lifted my T-shirt over my head. His eyebrows shot up in surprise as his eyes took in my form. My nipples pebbled under his stare. I wanted him. I always wanted him, no matter what was thrown our way.

"Are we okay?" My eyes locked with his, searching them as the fire sparked between us, binding us together.

"We're always okay, baby." He pulled me down onto his body and held me tightly, running circles up my back with his fingertips. He trailed his hands down my waist and slipped his fingers inside the waistband of my shorts. He fingered with the fabric before pulling it over my hips, taking my panties with them. I kicked them off my legs and lay against him, my naked body plastered against his partially dressed one.

"I need you," I murmured. "I need you now. I need you every night and every morning. I need us, always." Tears danced in my eyes as I bared my soul to him. I needed him to know how much I loved him, needed to show him the love I felt for him. He licked his lips and nodded before leaning up, twisting his hands in my hair, and pulling my lips to his own. He took my mouth passionately. Like he was thanking me for accepting him and his past. I loved him regardless of it all. I broke the kiss and pulled the sheet off his body before sliding his boxer briefs down his legs. He was hard and ready and when I palmed him, he twitched, lust sparking in his eyes.

I pulled up on my knees and held him in my hand, positioning him at my entrance before I sank down onto him. Tristan filled me—every corner and every fiber of my being hummed for him. Satisfied the constant yearning I had for him was being fulfilled at the moment, I rocked back and forth, taking him in and out of my body slowly, worshipping him and celebrating us. I moaned and ran my hands up the cut lines of his chest, his smooth skin beneath my hands, the rippling muscles working as we made love.

He took my breath away.

Every day he took my breath away and as long as I had him, I was okay with it. He could have it. Because he gave me back so much more.

Tristan's hands ran up my ribcage, lighting my skin on fire, causing lightning bolts of pleasure to pulse straight through to my core. I rocked and moaned, taking all the pleasure he was giving me. His hands palmed my breasts, brushing over my sensitive nipples. I gasped as I arched to his body. His hands snaked up my collarbone and laced around my neck, locking into my hair. He pulled me down onto him and kissed me with fierce passion. Tongues tangling and caressing, lips bruising, swallowed moans, and breathless pants echoing around the walls of the bedroom.

"Please don't leave me," he said softly between kisses. Tears sprang to my eyes and fell down my cheeks. I froze above him and pulled away from his lips to look at him. His eyes glistened in the moonlight and I could see the water that had pooled there.

"Oh no, no, Tristan." I held his beautiful face in my hands, searching for the right thing to say to take the pain from his eyes.

"I don't want this to be goodbye. I'm afraid you're telling me goodbye." He choked out the words, his eyes boring into mine.

"Never. I'm never saying goodbye. I couldn't if I tried. I love you so much more than I ever thought possible. I can't leave you. This," I placed my palm over my heart, "this beats for you. I can't live without my heart, and you have it." I prayed it was enough to ease his mind.

He only nodded, his hands at my hips holding me to him.

"Do you believe that?"

He licked his lips again and watched me. I could see his brain working as he processed my words.

"Tristan. It's true." I stroked his cheeks with my thumbs before leaning down and pressing my lips to his, taking him in a kiss, praying I could communicate all my love for him in one passionate, possessive action.

"My heart doesn't beat without you. You're stuck with me." I pulled away and grinned. His beautiful smile lifted at the corners and the twinkle returned to his eyes.

"There's no one else I'd rather be stuck with," he murmured and pulled my lips down to his again as he worked his hips against my own, restarting our passionate coupling. I moved with him even slower than before, cherishing our connection, not wanting to tear our lips apart.

"And just for the record, there's no one's ass I'd rather be stuck with." He nipped at my earlobe before turning us over in one smooth motion, holding my thighs high in his hands and plowing into me. I grabbed the headboard and clenched my fists around it, my head thrust back in pleasure. I moaned his name as he rocked into my body, hitting every sensitive nerve I had. My eyes flickered open as he thrust and I watched his hair fall over his forehead, his head bent down, watching where we connected: where our bodies came together, where I took him in with all the love I had. He sucked his bottom lip between his teeth and his hands tightened on my thighs. So tightly, it was nearly painful— so tightly, he would leave bruises just as he'd done that night last summer. It was like he was holding onto me for dear life, as if despite everything I'd told him, he was still afraid I would run.

"Fuck, Georgia. So close. Come with me. I need you to come with me." He groaned before his head shot up, eyes on me, lip still sucked between his teeth. My climax built in my core, the pressure becoming unbearable before it exploded over me like a freight train. Tristan thrust twice more before his whole body shuddered, a soft moan escaping his beautiful lips. His eyes fluttered closed, his hips slowed their rhythm, and he bent down, his beautiful body curved over me, his head on my shoulder and heated pants shaking his body. One palm trailed up my torso and curled around my neck, holding our heads together as he emptied into me. His hips finally stilled as he stayed inside me. I took everything he had to give. I was open to him and nothing could take me away, but I feared his own demons refused to let him see that.

I wondered if this would be our battle. He would always fear that I would leave, and I was afraid his past would forever haunt us.

Thirty

Georgia

"Mmm, come back here and warm me up," I heard Tristan groan as I peeled myself off his body to head for the bathroom.

"I can't hold it anymore." I squealed as he pulled me back onto his hard body and skimmed his hands up and down my back and torso.

"So tickling would be a bad idea?" He dug his fingers into my hips and I burst into a fit of giggles, writhing away from him.

"Mercy, God, mercy!"

His fingers slowed their assault, but he still held me to him. I finally quit laughing and looked up into his eyes. They sparkled and hummed with energy, but that heart-stopping smile he usually had when he was teasing me was absent.

"You're so fucking beautiful in the morning," he said

without an ounce of amusement on his face.

My cheeks flushed at the compliment. “I think you need to have your eyes checked.” I pushed away from him to head for the bathroom.

“Let’s get married,” he blurted.

“You already asked me that and, as I recall, I said yes.” I lifted my hand and spun the ring on my finger.

“No, let’s do it this weekend.”

“You’re serious?” I lifted my eyebrows in surprise.

“As a heart attack. Everyone we love is here. Let’s do it this weekend.”

I furrowed my brow as I considered his words. “I don’t want to rush it.”

“It isn’t a rush; I asked you the first time last winter. I wanted to marry you then and I want to marry you now. Nine months, I’d call that a pretty long engagement.”

“Not really. A lot of people plan a wedding for a year, or even two. Anyway, what about your dad?”

“He’s not really a wedding kind of guy. Come on, let’s do this.”

“Tristan, I told you I’d marry you. Give me time to plan a wedding.”

“You said yes three months ago and you still haven't chosen a date. No wedding planning in sight. Let’s do this, Georgia. Stop fucking around.”

My face dropped in shock. “You think I'm putting you off?” I whispered.

“I don’t know what you’re doing. What I know is you won’t give me a date to be my wife.” He deadpanned. The pain that had crossed his beautiful features last night was back.

“God, I’m not putting you off. I want to marry you. It’s just been so busy this summer, so many things have come up. I just wasn’t sure—”

“If you still wanted to?” His jaw worked back and forth, anger flashing across his stunning features.

I sat there, letting his words sink in, his hands digging into my hips, keeping me positioned on his body. I chewed my bottom lip into my mouth as I held his fiery gaze. I tried to get my thoughts together before I said something I didn’t mean.

“That was not what I was thinking. Now let me up to go the bathroom.” I pulled off his body, his arms falling away from my hips in defeat. I needed a minute to collect my thoughts. I headed for the bathroom and took care of business. Anger boiled in my stomach at his assumptions. I hadn’t put off the wedding planning because I didn’t want to marry him. I didn't *think* I'd done that anyway. I took a deep breath and tried to see things from his perspective.

He sat up in bed, perched against the headboard, his

fingers tapping a rhythm on his sheet-covered thigh when I exited the bathroom.

"Hey . . ." I slid up beside him and curled around his body, pressing my hands against his pecs and placing a sweet kiss on his lips. His eyes softened and his hands came around to envelop me in a calm embrace.

"I want to marry you, Tristan. You put this ring on my finger and that's it. You're not getting rid of me, not ever." I stroked my fingertips along the stubble at his jaw. "But I don't want to rush this. I'm afraid you're only saying this right now because you think I'm going to run with the whole Lexi thing, but I'm not—"

"That's not it. I don't think you're going to run because of that. I just . . ." He trailed off and diverted his gaze.

"You just what?" I angled his head back to me to meet my eyes.

"I'm scared. I'm afraid you're going to run because everyone runs on me. I was good all summer. I kept telling myself you wouldn't, but I'm afraid this Lexi thing may push you over the edge. And when you needed a girls' weekend . . . I just remember with Kyle that's how you started to pull away." He sucked his beautiful full lip between his teeth. My breath escaped in a soft whisper as I ran my thumb over the sculpted bow of his top lip and tugged his bottom one free.

"I'm not running. I'll always need a girls' weekend, and anyway, look how that turned out. Here I am, back in your bed."

"Our bed."

"Our bed." I smiled.

"I want to marry you because I want you to be my wife. Sooner rather than later." He slid a warm palm around my neck, his thumb working soft circles on my cheekbone.

"Yeah?" Tears sprang to my eyes as I watched the love pouring from him. He had so much love to give. He'd been cheated from his mother's love when he was little, but the love he held inside him overwhelmed me.

"Yeah." He brought his lips to mine in a soft kiss, his tongue caressing my lips, letting him once again own my heart.

"Okay." I pulled away from his lips, a smile lighting my face.

"Okay what?" His emerald green eyes searched my own.

"Okay, let's get married."

"This weekend?" His eyebrows shot up in surprise.

"We've been engaged long enough. I'm ready to make you mine." I grinned up at him. A heart-stopping smile lit his face. His teeth were on full display, lips curved up in a brilliant smile.

"God, you're so fucking beautiful." He threaded both his hands into my hair and crashed my lips to his. "I'm so fucking ready to tie myself to you forever."

"Thanks, I think." I laughed.

"Smart ass." He flipped me over and took my lips with his again, before moving along to my neck and across my collarbone. He discovered my body with his lips and his hands, skimming, sucking, caressing, and loving and it was the most beautiful wake-up call I'd had with him yet.

"Will you walk me down the aisle, Silas?"

"Georgia . . ." He leaned in and planted a kiss on my cheek. "It would be my honor." I could see tears swimming in his eyes. "Now let me see you." He held me at arm's length to inspect the lace dress that hugged my lean form. "This is way too old-fashioned, we need something sexier." He swatted me on my ass and I giggled before turning back into the dressing room. Drew, Silas, and I were at a local dress shop. I was forced to buy off the hanger, but I was glad to have a wedding dress at all after Tristan sprang his "let's get married right now" proposition on me.

The consultant zipped me into a flowing champagne-colored dress. I stepped out of the dressing room and onto the pedestal to take in my reflection in the three-way mirror.

"That's what I'm talking about. Spin." Silas turned his finger in circles.

"Oh my God, G." Drew stood with her hands locked to her lips, tears pooling in her eyes. "It's breathtaking."

"Really?" I turned in the mirror. "You think he'll like it?" I took in the short train before my eyes zeroed in on the intricate beadwork on the straps. They came together across my shoulder blades and then connected in a waterfall of lace and beadwork down the center of my spine to the small of my back where they attached to the champagne satin.

"He will be breathless, love."

"Yeah?" I turned, a smile curling my lips, tears swimming in my eyes as the overwhelming emotion came to the surface. I was marrying Tristan today. My heart thudded in my chest. I was excited, but didn't have a single second thought. I expected Drew and Silas to second-guess me, but instead they'd squealed and pushed me into the car to get a dress before our evening ceremony.

"*Ho Hey* by The Lumineers rang through the dress shop and Drew fumbled for her phone. "I have to take this, it's the officiant. But that's the dress. He's going to be hard for you all through the ceremony." She winked.

"Drew." I laughed before looking in the mirror again.

"And don't forget we have to swing by the town clerk's

office for a marriage license. You're going to be Georgia Howell," Drew sang, answering her phone.

"She's right. You're stunning, love." Silas stepped onto the pedestal with me and wrapped his arms around my waist, setting his chin on my shoulder.

We locked eyes in the mirror. "I love you, Silas. For everything. For being there for me, for being you, for making me laugh, for telling me how it is when I don't want to hear it."

"I love you too, Georgia." He swiped tears from his eyes. "Enough with the sappy shit. We've got a wedding to plan."

"Okay." I smiled softly. "Silas?"

"Yeah, love?" He turned to look back at me.

"Do you like him?" I whispered, my eyes searching his bright blue ones.

"I love him, Georgia. And more importantly, you love him. I can see it every time you look at him, and every time he looks at you. Even with everything going on, I knew you'd get through it. Do you think I'd let you marry just anyone?"

"No." I smiled and wiped a tear from my eyes.

"So why the sad face?" My best friend held my cheeks in his palms.

"It's just . . .the way we started . . ." I stopped as more

tears slid down my face.

"Hey, hey. Just because you started off ugly, doesn't mean you can't have a marriage that's just as strong and beautiful as everyone else's. Okay, love?"

I nodded as his words eased the fear in my heart.

"Good. Plus, he's nice to look at. I don't mind sharing holidays with that face."

"Silas, you're a married man." I sniffed the last of my tears away.

"You think Justin doesn't agree with me? We've got our list. We get a pass with anyone on our list, and your boy, if he ever goes bi, is on my list." Silas winked.

"Silas. Fuck, seriously? That's my future husband."

"I know." He shrugged.

"Would you really?" I arched a concerned eyebrow.

"Not for a minute. I'm just teasing you, love. But if I would have gotten hold of him a year ago . . ."

"Oh my God." I giggled and smacked him on the cheek. "You'll never change."

"You wouldn't have it any other way."

"Not for a second." I pecked him on the lips.

"Go change. We have to go to the flower shop and then Drew has big plans for us at home." He passed me a loving smile.

"I need to see her." I heard Tristan growl from the other side of the door.

"You can't see her before the wedding," Drew's voice replied, anger seething in every word.

"I don't care. I need to see her." I heard a scuffle.

"Tristan. You fucking caveman." I heard a thud and imagined it was Drew's fist meeting Tristan's solid chest.

"Babe?" A soft knock hit the door.

"Yeah?" I whispered.

"Can I come in?"

I licked my lips. I knew Drew was going to be pissed. We were less than a half hour away from the ceremony, my hair and makeup were done, and I was trussed up in a backless lace corset and garters, the last step before putting on my dress.

"Just a sec." I scurried, dress in hand, to hang it in the bathroom before closing the door so he wouldn't see it. "'Kay," I whispered as I stood in the middle of the room, waiting for him.

"Georgia," Drew shrieked. Tristan opened the door, ducking his head in, blond waves falling over his eyes. He was dressed in charcoal slacks and a white shirt, untucked but buttoned, a beautiful grey blue tie hanging loose around his neck.

"Five minutes," Drew ordered before Tristan shut the door in her face.

"Hey." His eyes held mine, his gaze hot and fierce. Passion simmered just beneath their emerald depths.

"Hey," I murmured. His eyes flicked down my body, over the lace hoisting my breasts to my chin, the boning whittling my waist, the scrap of lace panties and the garters attached at my thighs. He inhaled a sharp breath. I pressed my lips together nervously.

"Are you good?" he muttered as he stepped closer, taking my face in both of his hands.

"So good," I answered, never breaking his intense gaze.

"'Kay." He pressed his lips to mine in a kiss that meant so much more than just our lips pressed together. It conveyed his longing for me and anxiety that I still might run. I wouldn't run. Truth be told, I was surprised how calm I was. If anything, I was afraid he would cave, decide he wasn't ready after all.

"Are you good?" I pulled away and searched his face. His eyes flicked down to my lips, swollen from his kiss.

"I'm so fucking good." He pulled me to his lips again. One hand smoothed down my ribcage and held me tight to him at the waist. I snaked a hand around his hips and held him to me.

"I love you," I murmured as I rested my head on his shoulder and took a hit of my favorite scent. That ocean fresh scent that calmed me, soothed my nerves, made me feel at home.

"I love you too, baby. More and more every day." He threaded his fingers through the loose waves that trailed over one shoulder. "You look beautiful." He lifted my head and dusted his nose along mine.

"Thanks." I closed my eyes and enjoyed this moment before we got married. Our last *single* moment together. My mind ran through the last year and a half remembering the instant he stepped into the beach house kitchen last summer, and tipped his head at me, his eyes taking me in. Then he'd helped me cook dinner and swiped a blob of paint off my temple. He took my breath away then and he was still doing it now.

"Time's up." Drew knocked on the door.

"See you in twenty?" He pulled away from me, worry dancing in his eyes, his full bottom lip sucked between his teeth.

"I'll be the one in white." I grinned and traced my

thumb along his upper lip before freeing the bottom one from his grasp.

“Can’t wait.” He sighed before leaning down to capture my lips with his own. He held my cheeks firmly in his hands, his thumbs resting on my cheekbones, holding my face while he took my lips, something he’d been doing since the beginning of us. He owned me with that kiss. Possessing me, reassuring me, reassuring himself.

“See you, beautiful.” He pulled away, bringing my hand to his lips and placing a soft kiss on my knuckles.

“See you,” I breathed. His lips turned up in his beautiful, lopsided grin before he turned and whisked out of the room. He past Drew, and she gave him an angry glare. He only winked as he passed her.

“Stubborn bastard,” she murmured before stepping in and heading for the bathroom for my dress. I laughed as butterflies danced in my stomach. He was my stubborn bastard and I loved every single bit of him.

Thirty-One

Tristan

I held her hand firmly in my own as we sat at the table. Every moment of today, she'd taken my breath away.

When she'd walked down the makeshift aisle in the sand lined with petals to meet me at the end,

when she'd told me she promised to love me forever and said, "I do," and

when she kissed me, she left me breathless.

But it shouldn't have been a surprise, because every day since she'd entered my life a year ago, she'd been stealing my breath.

Now we sat outside at the table Drew had set up, covered in white linen, champagne glasses half full, candles flickering in the evening light. I had finally married the girl that had been stealing my breath from day one.

My fingertips worked small circles, fingering the satin of her dress high on her thigh. Seeing her in that white dress, walking toward me, I'd closed my eyes because she was the most stunning fucking thing I'd ever seen. I'd never imagined my wedding day, never thought I would get married, never cared to, but seeing her walk toward me, watching her give her life to me, promising to love me and let me take care of her, wake up with her every morning—the enormity of the moment nearly stopped my heart.

"I can't wait to peel this dress off you," I leaned into her neck and whispered in her ear.

"Tristan." She looked up at me with hooded eyes, biting her bottom lip. I knew that look. That was the look that told me she wanted me. She squirmed and pressed her thighs together. Another one of her signals. White dress or not, she always looked better naked, and we'd been putting on appearances all fucking day. The minute her lips locked with mine after we'd said, "I do," I had wanted her. I wanted to consummate our love. Show her she was mine and I was abso-fucking-lutely hers. Every inch of me, every beat of my heart belonged to her.

"Let's duck out of her. They won't mind," I murmured as I traced a fingertip up her thigh. "You look gorgeous, but I like you better naked," I growled. She turned me into an animal.

"Yes." I could see her chest heaving with labored pants.

"Fuck, you're wet already, aren't you?" I nipped at her

earlobe as a small moan escaped her throat.

"Come on." Gavin threw his cloth napkin at me. "Like we don't know what the fuck you're doing, man." He laughed as Drew shook her head and ducked under his arm, snuggling up close.

"I can't help it if I want to get this dress off her." I ran my nose up the delicate line of her neck and felt her shuddering beneath my breath.

"Remember how we were, honey? You can't blame them." Justin passed Silas a knowing look.

"Jesus, spare me the details," Drew groaned before she tipped the glass of champagne to her lips.

"All night." Silas grinned and then pressed a deep kiss to Justin's lips. A smile lit my face because I loved it when Silas fucked with Drew.

"Can we call it a night? I want to get my wife in bed," I murmured, swallowing the last of the champagne in my glass.

"Tristan," she chided.

I shrugged. "You guys are staying in the beach house, right?"

"Yep. Go on. We'll take these few things in so you guys can get started on your wedding night." Drew winked at Georgia.

"I can help." Georgia stood and I whipped my head

around to look at her. I couldn't stand another minute. I'd been suffering with a tent in my pants all through dinner.

"They can get it, babe." I tried to signal her with my eyes. She arched a knowing eyebrow at me before I stood up and clasped one of her hands in mine. "Trust me, they can get it," I growled in her ear.

"Problem, lover boy?" She palmed my dick through my pants and my hips jerked involuntarily. The air escaped my lungs in a whoosh.

"That's it. We're starting our wedding night now if I have to carry you over my shoulder to our bedroom."

She giggled and gave my cock a squeeze.

"Vixen." I tugged on her hand. The breeze whipped her thick chestnut hair around her shoulder as the wind carried her laugh and she looked back at our friends and gave a small wave. They whooped and hollered at us as we walked up the sand to the deck. I lifted her in my arms, the soft satin of her dress caressing my skin as she wrapped her arms around my neck and giggled. I thought the champagne had gotten to her.

"You're such a caveman sometimes," she murmured.

"You bring it out in me." I flashed the crooked grin that always had her melting in a puddle at my feet before I stepped across the threshold of our house for the first time as husband and wife.

"My caveman," she murmured as I crossed into our room and set her down in front of the bed. She nipped her lip between her teeth and looked up beneath hooded eyelids.

"God, that look, baby." My heart pounded in my chest. I traced a finger along her collarbone, ran it across her shoulder, and then gently turned her away from me. I slowly unhooked the tiny hooks on her dress and watched it pool at her feet on the floor. The sexy corset she was wearing accentuated the perfect curve of her ass, down to her creamy thighs. I ran my fingers down her soft legs and unsnapped the garters. They dropped as I ran my hands back up to her waist, dusting my fingers along the lace covering her pussy. She moaned and arched into me and my dick throbbed in my pants. I was so fucking hard for her; I'd been thinking about this moment all goddamned day.

I moved my fingertips to slowly unhook each hook of the corset before it dropped to the floor at her feet. I pulled her long hair around her neck and let it lay over one shoulder. She arched her neck and opened up to me. I leaned in and dusted my lips along her skin, over her shoulder, following the curve of her body.

"So beautiful. Every inch of you." I inhaled the skin beneath her ear, taking in her soft scent. "I can smell you, how turned on you are. You have no idea what it does to me." I thrust my aching hard-on into her ass to let her feel just how fucking turned on I was. A muffled groan escaped her throat as she arched her back and threaded her fingers into my hair from behind. I sucked on the skin beneath her earlobe before I slowly turned her to face me.

"I have something for you." I pulled back, a seductive grin lifting my lips.

"I know, and I'm ready and waiting." She pressed her open palm to my rock hard erection.

"I have something else." I shook my head and bent to the duffle bag under our bed where I'd been keeping something for her.

She smiled before taking the present from my hands and hooking a finger in the wrapping paper. She peeled the paper away and I watched her eyes as they rose in surprise, her mouth forming a perfect O, before she put one hand to her mouth.

"Tristan," the word escaped her lungs on a puff of air.

"It's the 1903 edition of *Tristan and Iseult*. I found it in Jacksonville before I came back here . . . I was just waiting for the right time . . ." I pressed my lips together, worrying them. Maybe this wasn't enough, maybe she had expected more.

"Oh, it's beautiful." Her hands ran over the worn fabric of the cover.

"Is it okay? I didn't know what I could get that would

mean enough. I always associated so much pain with the story after my mom left, but after last summer . . . those were some of the best moments, my best memories, reading with you on the beach . . ."

"Tristan, it's so perfect. I never told you, but *Tristan and Iseult* is what brought me back here, back to you . . ." Soft tears fell down her cheeks.

My eyes narrowed in confusion. "What do you mean?" I swiped tears from her cheeks with my thumb.

"I found the book in my bag, months later, and it all came back. Every moment we had. And Tristan and Iseult, how they'd denied each other and it ruined them. I knew I couldn't do it anymore. I'd been living in a daze before then, but seeing that book brought it all back, brought you back, and I knew I couldn't stay away anymore. I left the same day." Her dark chocolate eyes held my own.

I sucked in a quick breath and pulled her into my arms. Caressing her soft hair, murmuring in her ear how much I loved her.

"God, okay, enough." She giggled as she swiped at the tears in her eyes. "I don't have anything for you," she said softly.

"This," I yanked her hips flush with mine, my erection pressed between us, "is more than enough." I nipped the flesh beneath her ear.

"Well . . ." She pulled away. Her thumbs dusted across her hips as she slowly moved her panties back and forth. Her thumbs hooked into the delicate lace as she eased them an inch down, another inch. So fucking low before she stopped and turned, her lip sucked between her teeth. She was giving me a strip tease. Her tits were full, her nipples hard, and she was teasing me with that little scrap of panties. There was no way I could find the patience for this after waiting all day.

"Baby," I murmured as my eyes watched her thumbs playing with the lace at her hips. I growled before I lunged at her, dropping to my knees and tearing the lace off her body. I heard it tear, heard her giggle, but could think of nothing else but her intoxicating scent filling my nostrils. I brushed my nose in her pussy and lapped at her swollen folds. I licked and teased her clit. She clenched her fingers in my hair and tugged, pulling my face to her wet core, begging for more, as I tasted her. Devoured her. I was ravenous for her. I was a man on a mission and my mission was to have her come all over my face, repeatedly. Tonight.

"Tristan. Oh God, Tristan," she moaned as I felt her hips gyrating against my face. I wrapped my lips around her swollen clit and sucked and swirled my tongue, pulled it into my mouth, and sucked again. I scraped my teeth along her aching flesh before I thrust two fingers into her hot, wet pussy and pulled at her. She exploded around me, drenching my hand, her scent overpowering me. I sucked and felt her flesh throbbing around my fingers, milking me, her core hot and wet and quivering.

"So fucking beautiful when you come all over my face," I murmured before pushing her back on the bed and spreading her legs for me. I pushed my fingers through her swollen flesh and lapped at her, taking everything she had to give until she was clean. She writhed and moaned, her fingers kneading her breasts, her head thrust back in the most elegant way. I loosened my tie and threw it on the floor, shrugged my shirt over my shoulders, and paused to take her in. Her beautiful body lay out before me, curvy and soft and all mine. My hands ran up her torso and I plucked at her nipples, then wrapping around her neck, thumbs at her collarbone as she panted with pleasure.

"I want to see this face every day."

"What face?" she breathed as her eyes finally rolled open

"The face that says I've given you so much pleasure you've lost yourself."

"Oh," she murmured as she sucked her lip between her teeth.

"Don't hurt those beautiful lips either." I traced my tongue along the seam and they opened for me. I kissed her, devoured her, gave her the taste of herself on my tongue. She wrapped her arms around my neck, threaded her fingers in my hair, and held my body to her own. I felt so connected to her. A year ago, it would have scared me to feel that much for anyone.

But she wasn't just anyone.

She was my Georgia.

My girl, forever.

And despite anything we were going through, she'd given me that. My mind was at peace. I wasn't afraid she would leave me. The caveman in me sighed in relief. I had a ring on her finger, and she was in my bed. I knew I was the only one that could make her come undone like that. She was mine and she wasn't running.

"I want you inside me," she murmured as she locked her legs around my waist. I grinned against her lips as I fumbled with the button on my pants. She shoved them down my hips and my aching cock sprang free. I teased her wet folds, ran up the seam of her lips, and ground my pelvis into her clit. She gasped and then a low moan escaped her throat.

"Fuck, you drive me insane. Every moan, every look. I can't get enough," I murmured before thrusting deep into her. Her body lifted off the bed as she took me in, begging for the connection we always felt when we were together.

"Jesus, you're so wet," I muttered against her lips.

"Tell me," she murmured. I huffed a breath against her flesh, sucking on her sweet skin, tugging it between my teeth.

"I feel you throbbing around my cock. Sucking me in, begging me to take you. Your lips wrapping around my shaft. Your heels digging into my ass." This was her favorite, when I described every single sensation I was feeling.

"Faster, harder, please."

"No, baby. Nice and slow. I want to feel everything," I murmured as I dragged my cock in and out of her tight pussy. Drag and thrust, plunge and pull. Her breath picked up as I sucked an erect nipple into my mouth, her body arching off the bed, her heels pushing my hips into her throbbing core, pulling me deeper.

"Every smooth ridge, I can feel the end of you. Feel your pulse quickening around my dick. Your clit swelling against my pelvis when I grind into you," I whispered before shaking overtook her body, clenching my cock, her legs quivering, nails digging into my back as her release shot through her.

"I've waited, so long . . ." she murmured between pants.

"For what, baby?" Speech was difficult as I thrust in and out of her, hit the end, and swirled my hips, causing her to moan repeatedly. She was losing herself. Losing herself in the pleasure. I could see it in her eyes—the way her neck arched, the way her nails clawed at my back, my arms. She was ravenously seeking me.

"For you. I've been waiting so long for you," she murmured as I took her. My heart beat tenfold as my eyes widened at her words. I searched her beautiful face, held taut with ecstasy, her full lips red and swollen from my kisses. She pulled one elegant arm up behind her and held onto the bedpost.

There she was, taking my fucking breath away. The way she gave herself over to me. By giving me everything she had, she owned me. I'd told her that before, and I'd meant it, but today, giving me her future without question, our future was solidified. Everything snapped into focus.

Life with her.

Our kids.

Our grandkids.

She and I.

Coffee on the porch as the waves roared.

Watching the winter roll in on the beach.

Sailing in the summer.

My world shifted and now she was my axis.

I revolved around her.

I would do anything for her.

"You're my fucking heart, Georgia. My entire world. I was born to love you," I professed between thrusts as she began to clench around me again, the nails of one hand digging into my bicep, the pain radiating through my body, landing at my balls, before they drew up tight and I released into her. She came undone beneath me, screaming my name as the walls of her pussy throbbed around my already softening cock.

"I love you so much," she whispered as she threaded her fingers through my hair. I nuzzled at her neck, propping myself on one elbow as I relished her sated, limp, post-orgasm body. This was my favorite. Seeing her satisfied and dreamy, her eyes hooded, breathing short, limbs heavy. Knowing I had put the satisfied look on her face made me the happiest man on Earth. Knowing that she'd married me, the knowledge that I'd wake up to her each and every morning, made it that much better.

I hunched over her sweat-drenched body and sucked one of her delicate pink nipples into my mouth. I sucked and tugged and then released it with a soft kiss. I heard her heart pounding beneath her breastbone and placed a kiss there.

She was my fucking everything and I was going to show her that each and every day. A day would never go by where she questioned if I still loved her, still wanted her.

She deserved everything I had to give and so much more, and I'd spend the rest of my life showing her just that.

Thirty-Two

Tristan

"Up and at 'em, wife," I teased in the hollow of her throat. My warm breath spread across her skin, causing goose bumps to form. She sighed and stretched, a lazy grin spreading across her face before her eyes fluttered open, and she gazed back at me.

"Starting with that already?" One hand cupped my jaw and her thumb swept across my stubbled cheek.

"I like the way it sounds." I shrugged sheepishly.

"Me too," she said, all teasing gone from her voice. I dipped my head and placed a soft kiss on her lips, relishing the feel of them beneath mine.

"I need to take you on a honeymoon." I tugged her bottom lip between my teeth and pulled. Her eyes shut with desire as she wrapped both her legs around my naked hips, the sheets tangled between our bodies.

"Honeymoon?" she murmured as she nibbled on my earlobe.

"We're going for a sail."

"Won't it be cold?" She wrapped her locked ankles around my waist and pulled me tighter against her body. My dick pressed between us, throbbing with need for her as her hips ground circles against mine.

"Forecast looks great the next few days. I'll take you somewhere warm and tropical as soon as we can swing it, but I want to run away with you right now."

"What about everyone else?" Her brow furrowed as she referred to our best friends camped out in the house down the beach.

"They're leaving today anyway. They can lock up the house." I captured her lips with my own again and swirled my tongue inside her mouth, convincing her with my kiss to say yes.

"Okay," she murmured before I proceeded to worship my wife with my lips.

"So where we headed, Captain?" She curled up on the bench next to the captain's chair on the boat.

We'd gotten a little behind schedule—first our glorious lovemaking and then Drew had insisted on brunch before we all left. She'd promised they'd lock the house behind them before they left to go back to Jacksonville. Georgia had hugged her tightly, tears in her eyes. I made a vow to insist that Gavin and Drew and little Bennett come up more often and that we would visit Jacksonville whenever we could.

"North." I winked at her.

She narrowed her eyes at me. "I got that much. Any particular destination in mind?"

"Nope. We're just sailing. We've only got a few days, though. I thought we'd drop anchor when we're done for the day, sleep on the boat, then do it all over again the next day."

"Sounds cold and uncomfortable." She frowned as she picked at a thread on her sweater.

"I promise you, it will be neither of those things." I glanced over at her, taking her in. My mind remembered the first day I'd taken her on the boat over a year ago. The day that I'd let her steer and she'd fallen into me. She'd taken me by surprise, and I'd been willing to do anything to be in her presence.

She didn't know it, didn't get it—hell, *I* didn't get it—but I was happy as fuck she'd let me have her.

Chosen me.

That's what she'd done.

She'd finally chosen me and I now felt at peace with us.

No more worrying that she would run, that I wasn't worthy. I'd made myself worthy of her, done everything I could to get us here. Waited for her, stopped fucking around, settled myself. Pushed her, but never too far. She was here and I was here and we'd chosen each other and it was the most comforting feeling on Earth.

Thirty-Three

Tristan

We returned Wednesday afternoon. I'd dropped Georgia off at the grocery store to buy some food for dinner and ran to the post office. I grabbed the large stack of mail that'd accumulated after days away and crawled back into the Jeep. I sifted through the stack: bills, junk mail, something from *Greater North Carolina Testing Services.*

My heart shuddered to a halt.

My palms prickled and turned white as I clutched the innocent-looking white envelope in my hands. I couldn't catch my breath.

I shouldn't open this here. Not without her. I didn't want to shatter the blissful bubble we'd been in the first few days of our marriage. I didn't know what these test results said, and I wasn't sure what I wanted them to say, but either way, it would affect us somehow.

I tossed the remaining mail on the console between the

seats and turned the key. I drove in a semi-daze to the grocery store to get my girl. I sat in the parking lot, fingering the letter while Charlie panted obnoxiously in the back seat. I flipped it between my hands, my fingers worrying the edges. I pulled my lips between my teeth and tapped my fingers on the steering wheel. Charlie stood in the back, placed his two big paws on the console, and panted hot, heavy breaths in my face.

"Fuck, come on, Charlie." I ducked my head away and rolled down the window for fresh air. "Should I wait for her?" I tapped the letter against the steering wheel. Just then, the back door opened and Georgia shoved a multitude of bags into the back seat.

"Thanks for the help. What the hell are husbands good for if they can't carry the groceries?" she mumbled before settling herself in the front seat and locking her seatbelt.

"Sorry." I turned to her. Taking in her face, the chocolate waves of her hair. Her beautiful full lips curved in a pout, melted chocolate eyes watching me, the delicate eyebrows arched in surprise.

"What? Is something on my face?" She swiped at her mouth before pulling down the mirror.

"No," I muttered before leaning into her. "Thank you for marrying me." I kissed her lips chastely.

"Oh." Her mouth formed that adorable O and I couldn't

help but smile at her surprise and innocence.

"I picked up the mail." I pulled my lips between my teeth again and averted my eyes.

'"Yeah?" I could feel her eyes still watching me.

"This came." I thrust the offending letter at her. The one that had my stomach in knots.

She flipped it over and read the return address. "Oh." Her face fell with understanding. "You didn't open it yet?"

"No, I was waiting . . . I guess . . ." I trailed off.

"Okay. Do you want me to . . . ?" she offered.

I shook my head feverishly. "No, let's just have dinner first. Get settled." I started the Jeep and pulled out of the parking lot, steering us toward home.

"This is driving me nuts. I can't watch you like this. It's like pulling off a band aid—just open it." She stood from the kitchen table an hour later, taking both of our plates to the sink. She swiped the envelope off the island and thrust it at me. I chewed on my bottom lip, ran a hand through my hair, and shuffled my feet. My heart felt like it was lodged in my fucking throat. This was the moment where I'd find out if Trevor were mine. If I had a son. If I'd had a baby with someone else, and my new wife was here watching me, supporting me, loving me, regardless of the results. It meant the entire fucking world to me that she'd married me without even knowing the results. She'd proven it didn't matter, she loved me anyway. Loved me enough to stay, regardless. That single act had proven to me I was enough in her eyes.

"Can you do it?" I looked up at her, my eyes round as saucers, pleading with her to take some of my anguish away.

"Yeah, baby." She pulled herself into my lap and threaded her hands in my hair, scratching my scalp, placing a soft kiss along my neck, calming me. "No matter what it says, things are going to work out exactly as they were meant to, okay?" Her soft brown eyes held mine and I nodded. "Okay." She pulled the envelope from the table as I tapped my fingers against her lower back nervously.

She tugged the end open, ripping the stark white paper before sliding out the small stack of results. She looked the papers over and I watched her eyes dance across the first few sentences. She sucked in a sharp breath and read a few more, moisture filling her eyes before she laid the papers in her lap and looked over to me.

Her eyes bore into mine. Searching for answers, my eyes widened, waiting for what she would tell me about my future.

If I were Trevor's dad.

I loved the kid; had gotten the chance to know him these last few months. I wanted to give kids to Georgia, share that with her, just us, but I also knew there was a small piece of my heart that was attached to the four-year-old boy who'd shown up on my porch this summer.

"He's not . . . the results are negative. You're not his dad." Tears trickled down her cheeks as she wrapped me in her arms. I sat frozen for a minute, my heart pounding in my chest. It ran so fucking fast, I thought it would burst out of my ribcage and gallop off.

I wasn't Trevor's dad.

Trevor wasn't mine.

He looked like me, had my eyes, but that was coincidence. I wrapped my arms around Georgia and, finally, a sigh escaped my lips. "I don't know what to think." I held onto her for dear life. If there was anyone I needed at this moment, it was her, in my arms. In my life. "I didn't want him to be mine for you . . . but I think part of me did want him," I murmured so softly it was a revelation to me.

"I know. I know," she whispered as she stroked my back.

"I didn't think I was ready to be a dad, but when he looked up at me . . . I want kids, Georgia."

"I know, honey. Buckets full," she whispered, a smile in her voice.

"I want kids now." I pulled away, gazing at her.

"Now?" Her eyebrows knit together. "You're probably just adjusting. You thought for so long he was yours and now to find out he's not . . ."

"No, that's not it. Being his dad, no matter how short, I loved it. And I want that. With you." I held both of my hands against her flat stomach. Her eyes darted down to my hands holding her belly. I knew what she was thinking, because I was thinking it too. I was thinking about my child; our baby growing inside her. She licked her lips before her eyes found mine again.

"Yeah?" she whispered, her lips parted slightly as small breaths escaped them.

"Yeah." I grinned. "I want to get started on those buckets full of babies," I murmured before I kissed her and laid her down on the floor, worshiping her body in the best way I knew how because Georgia had finally chosen me.

Chosen this.

Chosen us.

Epilogue

Tristan

"Uhm . . . what the fuck are you doing?" I stepped out of the bathroom, my eyebrows scrunched together as I took in Georgia's form on the bed, a pillow propped under her ass, legs in the air.

"Shut up," she pouted. "It helps your swimmers get to where they need to be."

"Seriously?" I cocked my head to the side, an eyebrow arched in disbelief.

"I read it. You would know that too if you would have read the daddy book I bought you, you jackass." She laughed before fumbling for a thick blue and pink baby book on the nightstand and whipped it at my head.

I caught it before it had a chance to take me out. "Babe, I don't think my swimmers need any help." I winked at her, setting the book back on the nightstand and standing beside her contorted form on the bed.

"Well, dear, my eggs may say otherwise since it's been

three months since we started trying . . ." Her voice trailed off, water misting her eyes.

"Georgia . . ." I sat beside her on the bed and threaded my fingers through her long, chocolate locks. "It's gonna happen for us, baby, just give it time. Can't stress affect it? We had so much going on over the holidays. Just give things some time to calm down." I dusted a kiss along her temple.

"Yeah, but what if I can't have kids? What if I'm barren? I've been on birth control for years, Tristan. *Years*. Maybe that makes a person sterile long-term." She wiggled her hips and arched her ass farther in the air.

"Did you read that somewhere?"

"No, but—"

"No buts. It'll just take time." I placed a soft kiss on her cheek before pulling on a pair of jeans that were lying in a heap on the floor.

I was about to head to the porch to call Trevor for our Saturday morning sports recap. After we'd gotten the paternity test results and found out that I wasn't Trevor's dad, I'd called Lexi and we'd talked for a long time. It broke my heart to explain to Trevor that I wasn't technically his dad, but that I still wanted to hang out with him. Apparently, the only other guy that could be his biological dad had problems with drugs and alcohol so Lexi didn't want him in

Trevor's life. I agreed with her, and I'd grown attached to the little guy, so I promised to swing by and see him whenever I was in Jacksonville and continue to call him at least once a week.

"Can't it take up to a year for your system to readjust without the birth control anyway?" I tried to ease her mind as I shrugged a button down over my shoulders.

"Yeah." She heaved a sigh. My hands dropped to my sides before I could button the shirt. She was so adorable, her eyebrows furrowed with worry, her legs hiked up, only a sheet covering her soft body.

Happiest day of my life when she'd said yes.

"Stop worrying, beautiful." I bent to kiss her.

"Come down here and keep me company. I have to sit like this for thirty minutes."

I rolled my eyes at her refusal to accept my reassurances. "I'm telling you, my swimmers? Strong. They don't need the help. But I will lie in bed next to your hot little body." I grinned and tweaked her nipple as I rolled onto the bed with her.

"Ow. You're a sadist." She grabbed her breast and massaged it in her hand.

"By all means then, let me help." I lowered my head, hair falling across my forehead, and sucked her little pink nipple between my lips, caressing it with my tongue, pulling on it, and drawing it out.

"Ugh," she whimpered and held my head to her chest.

"Ready again, baby?"

"Thirty minutes," she moaned. Jesus Christ, she was determined to follow that book, no matter what.

"Might help our chances to double the dose of swimmers." I grinned and sucked her other nipple into my mouth.

"Mmm . . . I don't think that's how it works," she whispered as she threaded her fingers in my hair and I got lost in her all over again.

"You're thinking about adopting?" I heard Georgia murmur over the phone. She sat perched on a deck chair, the misty air swirling her brown locks around her shoulders as she talked with Silas on the phone. I watched her from the French doors, listening in on her conversation.

We'd been married for six months, and been trying for a baby since the first night we'd gotten home from our honeymoon, without luck. I knew that every month that passed she grew sadder and sadder. She was becoming more affected by our inability to conceive and it ripped my heart out to watch her sadly shuffle into the room and announce that she'd gotten her period yet again.

She was losing heart.

Every month, we tried when she was fertile, but that wasn't the only time we were having sex, because we were still as insatiable as ever. I couldn't get enough of her, but now, during her fertile window, she went to great lengths to encourage the swimmers, as she said. I tried to make a joke, tried to make it a laughing matter, but I could tell the humor was slowly leaving her.

The thing she'd always dreamed of, the life she'd always wanted, and we were having trouble making it happen. I'd already gone to the doctor to see if it was me. I'd splooged in a cup, nervous that it could be my fault that we hadn't yet made a baby. The counts had come back good. Motility perfect. I prayed to God this wasn't a permanent problem, I didn't know if Georgia could deal with something else being taken away from her.

"Hey, babe. How's Silas?" I wrapped one arm around her as she tucked herself into me. She nuzzled into my neck and took a deep breath. Scenting me, taking me in, she'd been doing exactly this since the beginning and it made me delirious with love and desire for her.

"Good. He and Justin are thinking of adopting."

"Yeah? That would be great. They'd be great dads."

"Yeah . . . I just wish it wasn't so hard for us . . ."

"I know, Georgia." I'd stopped telling her to give it more time because truth be told, I wasn't sure that was all it would take anymore. I was scared that there was something wrong and that thought made my heart ache.

"Happy birthday, man." Gavin swatted me on the shoulder, beer in hand. Bennett ran full tilt across the living room and out the French doors, Charlie hot on his heels. His laughter echoed on the wind as Georgia and Drew giggled at his antics.

"Thanks." I tipped my beer to my lips. The start of the summer season: May, my birthday, and the time of year that business ramped up for the beach house. This day was usually hard for me, but since Georgia had come into my life, it had become something different. Something worth celebrating when she was here.

Drew and Gavin had married on Valentine's Day. They were spending the weekend with us. Silas mixed cocktails in the kitchen while Justin chatted with the girls outside. Our perfect little extended family. Silas and Justin had decided to move along with trying to adopt and were looking at a beautiful little girl from Romania.

"Presents," Georgia called as she motioned me over to

the kitchen table that was set up with gifts. I rolled my eyes because somehow this felt less like a thirty-year-old's party and more like one for a ten-year-old. I indulged her, though. She loved this stuff.

"This is great." I grinned as I opened a kit to make your own beer at home.

"Such a guy gift." Drew rolled her eyes and rubbed her belly. Soon after they'd gotten married, she'd found out they were pregnant again. Some people were just more fertile than others, I guessed. I'd watched Georgia's face falter when Drew had told her over the phone, but she'd been enthusiastic for her friend. "Open the envelope," Drew instructed.

"Aw, guys, this is great. Season tickets for the Pirates, baby."

"Great." Georgia rolled her eyes. I smacked her on the ass because I knew she secretly enjoyed going to baseball games with me. She loved going to the ball game, throwing a cute little ball cap on her head, scarfing hot dogs and drinking beer with me.

"Maybe I'll bring Silas, then."

"Not a chance, lover boy." Silas shook his head.

"Open ours." Justin stepped into the room from the deck, carrying a box. I narrowed my eyes when I heard a whine escape it. All the faces in the room lit up, including

Georgia's.

I opened the flaps and a tiny golden retriever puppy leaped out at me, all oversized paws and slobbering tongue.

"A puppy? Charlie's not going to like this." I lifted him in my arms and let him kiss me square on the lips. I was a sucker for dogs and now that Charlie was getting older, he did much more sleeping than anything else.

"Charlie gave his approval." Georgia bent to pet the old dog's head as he sat at her hip. He'd grown attached to her. I thought they'd bonded this past year. He probably appreciated that she was his excuse to bow out of morning jogs with me.

I set the puppy down and he instantly spotted Diva and charged off down the hallway after her.

"Diva, on the other hand . . ." Silas laughed as my eyes darted to Georgia.

"She can hold her own with all these boys." A laugh that lit my heart escaped her lips. Our plan for a baby might not have been working out, but I was deliriously happy, we were deliriously happy with the little life we had.

"Mine." She handed me a gift bag stuffed with entirely too much tissue paper. I dug and dug, pawed through it some more before lifting a tangled black contraption with straps and hooks.

"A sex swing? Babe, how did you know?" A grin spread

wide across my lips.

"You hornball." She swatted me on the ass. "Look at the tag." I kissed her on the lips. She bent her body into mine, swaying on her feet slightly as she ran a hand through my hair.

"God, still? I thought the expiration date on the honeymoon phase was up by now?" Silas muttered.

"Not anytime soon." I grabbed the cheek of her ass and goosed her for his benefit.

"Look at the tag, baby," she murmured against my lips. I pressed one last kiss there before turning the contraption over in my hands. My brows furrowed as I tried to discern what I was looking at.

"Happy birthday, baby." She rubbed a palm up and down my back. My breath caught in my throat. A lump formed the size of Texas.

"What is this?" I finally managed to ask.

"A baby carrier," she whispered. "We're gonna have a baby."

My heart stuttered to a standstill and my eyes widened as the carrier dropped from my hands and I turned to her. "You're pregnant?" I whispered as my eyes searched hers for any trace of misunderstanding. She only nodded, a beautiful smile breaking across her face as tears flooded her eyes.

"Jesus, we're going to have a baby?" I ran a hand through my hair in confusion and stress and worry and happiness. So many emotions. But the most beautiful of all was love for the beautiful girl standing beside me, whose dream was finally coming true.

"We made a baby?" I murmured and placed my hands to her stomach. "You're carrying my baby?" I dropped to my knees and lifted the hem of her shirt, pressing a kiss to her soft skin.

"Welcome to the club, Daddy. It killed me not saying anything," Gavin said.

"Wait, you knew? Did you all now?"

"You know she wouldn't keep it to herself." Drew grinned while Bennett squirmed in her arms.

"And this one couldn't keep it from me." Gavin swung an arm over her shoulder.

"I wanted to make it special," Georgia whispered from above me.

"God, no matter what, baby, it would have been special, but you're right, this is . . . perfect." I planted another kiss on her stomach before standing to wrap her in my arms.

"Again? Jesus, you're an animal."

She giggled as she slithered up my body and straddled my hips. "It's the pregnancy hormones. I can't help it." She whined before bending and snagging my lips between her teeth.

"Ow, Jesus."

She pulled away and my lips turned down in a pout.

"Has the situation reversed itself Mister Hornball? If you're turning down morning sex, I'll gladly take matters into my own hands." She pulled away with a smirk and ran her palm down the center of her body to the apex of her thighs.

"Never," I growled before lunging at her. She giggled and writhed underneath me as I traced my lips up her neck, sucked on her earlobe, and rocked my morning wood into her. "You know mornings are my favorite," I whispered before tugging one of her nipples between my teeth.

"Baby," she shrieked and yanked away, her hand massaging her breast. "They're sensitive."

"I'm sorry," I murmured before nudging her hand away and sucking her nipple into my mouth and caressing it delicately. She moaned and arched into me and I lost my head to desire. My hands skimmed down her torso and hiked one thigh around my waist as I probed at her entrance. I eased into her slowly as the sensation aroused me. She was so snug and warm, she fit me perfectly. Sent me straight to

Heaven when I was inside her.

"Faster, please, Tristan," she moaned as I locked my arms on either side of her body. I dragged in and out slowly, relishing the feel of her around me, watching her chocolate brown hair sprayed across the pillow, her bottom lip snagged between her teeth, eyes shut tightly as soft groans escaped her throat.

My hand traced down her ribcage and landed at the bump at her stomach. Five months pregnant, halfway and she was finally starting to show. The enormity of what we'd made, what our love had created inside her, amazed me. It left my brain scrambled in awe. There was a baby inside her. She carried my baby within her every day. He or she slept to the rhythm of her heartbeat, heard her beautiful laugh, was between us, literally, when we made love.

"What's wrong?" she breathed, her lust-filled eyes fluttering open. I swallowed the lump in my throat and glanced up at her. My heart hammered in my chest.

"The baby. Are you okay? Do you feel okay? I don't want to be too rough."

"Oh, baby, you won't be." She snaked a palm around my neck to cup my cheek. The pad of her thumb caressed my cheekbone. I closed my eyes and inhaled. "Hey, I promise I will tell you if you're being too rough, but you're not." She hooked her legs around my waist and locked her ankles, taking me deeper inside her.

"Georgia, what if . . . this is weird. I feel like I'm going to hit the baby . . . with my . . ." I couldn't finish the words—there was a baby in the room. Gone were words like cock and dick, replaced with innuendo. This baby had me turned on my head and it wasn't even out yet.

"Really?" She cocked an amused eyebrow at me.

"I dunno. It's weird."

"I thought you read the baby book? Sex is safe."

"I did, cover to cover. But it's still weird." I moved a little inside her, testing the waters. "Shit, what if I could feel the baby move from inside you? On my . . ." I arched an eyebrow in question.

"Oh my God, you are so ridiculous. Are you going to make me get myself off?"

"Never, not while I'm around. I want every orgasm from this point on. If I'm with you, only I'm getting you off." I moved in and out of her again.

"Good. Now fuck me like you mean it." She grinned. I couldn't refuse those words.

"You want it hard and fast?" I hiked her thigh up around my waist, thrust into her, and rolled my hips.

"Please," she moaned, "but watch the nipples."

"Got it, easy on the nipples." I pulled her legs up straight and over my shoulders and hit her to the very end, setting a punishing pace as I fucked her to the sound of her moans and pleas echoing around the room.

"Tristan," she shrieked from our bedroom. I flew out of my office and into our room. I saw her standing in the shirt she'd slept in, a pair of panties in her hand and a puddle of water on the floor.

"Fuck," I whispered and stood stock-still. I couldn't move. My heart hammered, my eyes as wide as saucers.

The baby was coming today.

The baby was coming now, and my brain couldn't process what I needed to do about it. Wrigley galloped into the room. The puppy, who was much less puppy and much more gangly dog, made his way to Georgia and sniffed the puddle on the floor.

"Tristan. Don't let him, oh my God," she moaned as she swatted at the dog to shoo him away. "Don't just stand there. Get my bag, get me a towel, call Drew!" Georgia was flipping out just like I was. Bad news. We both couldn't be flipping out. I was relatively sure two adults who had no idea how to raise a baby was bad news. Fuck, maybe we were in over our heads on this one. We could hardly wrangle two dogs and a high-maintenance cat.

"Tristan."

"Fuck, yeah, okay. Towel." I ran into the bathroom and pulled a towel from the rack.

"Not a good one," she squealed.

"Right. A bad one. Okay." I pulled an old towel from under the sink and threw it on top of the puddle between her legs.

"Hey," she called to me. I looked up at her, concern etched across my face. "It's going to be okay," she whispered and pressed a soft kiss to my lips. I sighed as she ran her fingers through my hair. I laid my forehead against hers and breathed in the vanilla scent of her, calming my nerves.

"Are you ready to have a baby, Daddy?" she murmured against my lips.

"As ready as I'll ever be."

"Good. Now let's get to the hospital."

"Right." I kissed her again. I felt centered. She did that to me. Had that calming effect. I picked up her overnight bag as she pulled a pair of leggings on and we headed out the door and to the hospital to have our baby.

"One more push, baby, just one more and the baby will

be here." I coached her from the top of the bed. The doctor sat between her legs, Georgia practiced her breathing as she pushed with every ounce of strength she had in her.

My wife blew my mind.

I was in awe of the strength she mustered to bring our baby into the world. A year and a half into our marriage, and she was still taking my breath away.

A loud cry pierced the room.

"It's a boy! Good job, Mama."

"He's here? Oh, Tristan," she whimpered as tears fell down her cheeks.

"You did so good, baby." I swiped the hair off her forehead and pressed my lips to her damp skin. "You did so good."

"Want to cut the cord, Daddy?"

My eyes widened in fear.

"Come on." The doctor waved me over, my squirming boy in her hands. I took the scissors from the nurse and cut where she instructed. Anxiety and happiness in equal parts chocked my throat as I realized that I'd just severed the tie that had connected him to his momma, my beautiful wife. She'd sustained him for all those months, held him in her body and cherished him in her heart and now it was my turn.

"Perfect. Want to hold your son before we start his

tests?"

I only nodded. I couldn't force the words from my lips.

The doctor pushed the baby into my arms and I stared down into his beautiful little face. Round cheeks and grey eyes, a button nose and thc most beautiful little bow-tie lips. Georgia's lips. My son had Georgia's lips and a fine layer of blond hair. He was ours. A perfect mixture of us.

I swallowed the lump that had formed in my throat. My whole body shook as I held my son and took in his beauty.

"Hey, little guy, we've been waiting so long for you." I placed a kiss on his head. I sucked in a long breath and inhaled him just like Georgia did me. I took him in, made him mine.

He owned me.

His little face owned me completely.

"Baby," I whispered as I brought him to Georgia. "He's got your lips." Tears filled my eyes and trailed down my cheeks as I laid him in her arms. "He looks like you, baby."

"Hey, sweetheart." She kissed his little head and his dark little eyes stared up at her face, took her in, recognizing her voice.

She captivated him just like she did me.

He needed her to breathe, just like I did.

Neither one of us ever stood a chance. From the moment we'd laid eyes on her, she owned us both.

"Can you change Brady's diaper?" she called from down the hall.

"I had the last one," I yelled as my eyes trained back on the football game.

"Babe, I can't change the diaper, seriously. It will make me sick," she whined as she stepped into the room, Brady wiggling in her arms in only a diaper.

"Shouldn't he be potty trained by now anyway?" I groaned as I stood from the couch.

"He's only eighteen months old, so no." She thrust my boy into my arms.

"Jesus," I held his stinky self at arm's length.

"Come on, buddy, don't you want to use the toilet like a big boy?"

"No." Ah, there it was, *no*, one of the few words he knew and used excessively.

"What a bum deal if you're going to be like this the whole pregnancy," I grumbled as I headed down the hall and into the nursery.

"It's just the beginning that my nose is so sensitive." She rubbed her tummy softly.

"Better be. If your nose is so sensitive, how is it you're

able to stand in here with me while I change the diaper?" I arched an eyebrow at her.

"It's just standing right over it I can't take." She wrinkled her nose and darted out of the room as a grin split across her face. I had a feeling she was bullshitting me about the sensitive nose thing. I knew she was sensitive to smells, coffee for one, but this dirty diaper sensitivity was way too convenient.

Lucky for her, I didn't care. I knew she had it rough, carrying a baby while a toddler ran around the house, leaving mass chaos in his wake. If I had diaper duty for the rest of the pregnancy, I was okay with that; it was the least I could do after watching her push our son into the world. That didn't mean I wasn't going to give her a hard time about it, though. I couldn't let her know she owned me so completely and could walk all over me, and I'd still have a smile on my face. Georgia did that to me. Got her way in all things and I happily gave it to her, gave her everything, because she'd given me everything.

Georgia

“Come on, boys, let’s go,” I called from the beach.

“Where’s Daddy and Brady?” My beautiful little girl looked up at me, golden ringlets pulled into a ponytail, dark brown eyes dancing with excitement.

“They’re coming, baby.” I patted her head just as Tristan and our four-year-old came bounding down the deck stairs of the beach house.

“Be careful,” I called, but I knew they couldn’t hear.

“Mama.” Brooke tugged on the hem of my cover-up.

“Yeah, baby?”

“Up.” She reached her chubby little arms up for me to hold her. A smile slid across my face as I heaved her into my arms. I looked back at my boys as they reached the bottom of the stairs. Tristan heaved Brady up on his shoulders and jogged to me, a beautiful smile crossing his face. My heart stuttered to a stop because it was just as I'd imagined in my daydream so many years ago. That summer we'd first met and I'd seen beautiful little blond-haired babies in the sand, a smiling Tristan entertaining them.

“Hey, Mama.” My gorgeous husband pressed a kiss to my lips. I adjusted Brooke on my hip and weaved a hand up to hold his cheek as I kissed him.

“Hey,” I whispered.

“You look beautiful,” he murmured as he pressed his forehead to mine.

"Thanks." I took his lips with mine again.

"Daddy, I'm ready to swim." Brady shook the bucket of beach toys in his hand.

"He's ready to swim, Daddy." I smiled sweetly.

"While they're swimming, can I get some alone time with my girl?" He quirked an eyebrow suggestively.

"Wait till nap time, Mr. Howell." I pulled away, but not before pinching his ass.

"Ow."

"What, Daddy?" Concern crossed our little boy's face.

"Mommy pinched Daddy."

"You shit," I whispered under my breath as Tristan's eyes gleamed with amusement.

"No pinching, Mommy," Brady chastised from atop Tristan's shoulders.

"Sorry, baby. Let's go swim." I darted off down the beach with Brooke squealing with delight in my arms. I set her down in the sand and she immediately started digging as the waves lapped at her chubby little feet.

"I'll be out in a minute." Tristan lifted Brady from his shoulders. Brady headed for his sister and plopped down, showing her how to make a sandcastle with the toys.

Tristan wrapped his arms around my waist and swayed me back and forth as he tucked his nose into my neck. I sucked in a contented breath and lay back against his chest.

"Thank you," I sighed.

"For what?" His lips tickled the skin beneath my ear.

"For everything. All of it. From the beginning to the end, thank you."

"Mmm, my pleasure, ma'am," he said in his best southern drawl.

"Seriously. Buying this house? Best decision I ever made." I turned in his arms and caught his gaze with my own. "That first day sailing? I'm so thankful you asked me and I said yes. Every minute I'm thankful for, even the hard ones." Tears pricked behind my eyelids, as I looked at the beautiful boy that had been stopping and restarting my heart from the moment I'd met him.

"Oh, baby." He kissed me softly. "Thank you, for bringing me back to life. For making this beat." He put my hand on his heart. "It beats for you and them." He gestured toward our babies playing in the sand.

I nodded and tucked my head into the crook of his neck. I inhaled deeply and took in his ocean fresh scent that had made my knees weak from the start. His lips whispered along my jaw line as he placed soft kisses across my skin.

"I love you," I murmured.

"I love you so much more," he replied before his lips took mine in a reverent kiss.

There he went again, stealing my breath, except he

wasn’t stealing it; I gave it to him freely because he owned me. We owned each other.

From the beginning, our lives had been set on a course to find each other. There'd been no deviating. Despite the bumps in the road, it’d gotten us here, and here was so good.

Here was the best.

Here was right where we were meant to be.

The End.

If you enjoyed Light in Mourning *please consider leaving a review. Reviews are like gold and I'll gladly send each and every one of you a cupcake in thanks, or a picture of a boy without a shirt, whichever you prefer* ;)

Stay tuned for a excerpt from *Love in Between* by Sandi Lynn.

Playlist

Madness ~ Muse

Animal ~ Neon Trees

Everything I Ask For ~ The Maine

Locked Out of Heaven ~ Boyce Avenue

Kiss Me Slowly ~ Parachute

She is Love ~ Parachute

Wherever You Will Go ~ Boyce Avenue

Falling ~ The Civil Wars

Stupid Boy ~ Keith Urban

If I Knew ~ Bruno Mars

It Will Rain ~ Bruno Mars

Love Remains the Same ~ Gavin Rossdale

I Won't Give Up ~ Jason Mraz

Safe & Sound ~ Taylor Swift, The Civil Wars

Between the Raindrops ~ Lifehouse

This Years Love ~ Boyce Avenue

Who You Are ~ Jessie J

I Choose You ~ Sara Bareilles

Find this playlist on *Spotify* along with more songs that inspired *Light in Mourning.*

Acknowledgements

Thank you to my loving and supportive hubs. Frozen food and dirty laundry have become a common occurrence in our house so I can write books. Our family has sacrificed, but hopefully the rewards are that much sweeter.

To the best sisters a girl could ask for—my SmutSisters. For all the support, love, boys without shirts (and sometimes without pants), laughs, and TMI conversations. My day isn't complete until I've chatted with you girls. Bring on Scotland!

To Nelle, you've become such a close and supportive friend. We growl about how tough it is to write books and dish about family and life; you're a blessing.

To Sandi, I have a blast chatting and bitching and beta-reading with you. I can't wait for all the signings in 2014!

And eternal thanks to my awesome, hilarious, and always supportive readers who love Tristan just as much as I do! You guys rock! I appreciate each and every message and review you so happily share!

About the Author

Adriane Leigh was born and raised in a snowbank in Northern Michigan and now lives among the sand dunes of the Lake Michigan lakeshore.

She graduated with a Literature degree but never particularly enjoyed reading Shakespeare and Chaucer.

She is married to a tall, dark and handsome guy and is mama of two sweet baby girls. Also a voracious reader and knitter.

Like facebook.com/LaceSeries

or

Follow @AdrianeLeigh on Twitter for regular updates on life, love, and writing.

Check out Goodreads to see what I'm reading.

More from Adriane Leigh

Steel and Lace

The Mourning After

Light in Mourning

Wild (December 2013)

Please enjoy an excerpt from *Love in Between* by Sandi Lynn.

Prologue

"You're the most beautiful bride that I've ever seen."

"You have to say that; you're my mom." I smiled.

I stared at my white A-line strapless dress, embellished with rhinestone flowers that cascaded asymmetrically over the bodice as I ran my hands down my sides. I turned my head to make sure my cathedral bridal veil was placed perfectly amongst my elegant curly updo.

"I can't believe you're finally getting married!" Giselle smiled.

"You're picture-perfect, Lily Gilmore," Gretchen said as she snapped a picture with her phone.

I was so nervous; my hands were beginning to sweat. I couldn't believe this day had finally arrived. The past year of planning the perfect wedding was torturous, but exciting. Hunter stood by my side and had agreed with everything that I liked. I think he just wanted to keep the peace, or he just didn't care. He didn't want a big wedding; he wanted to run off to Vegas and get married at one of those drive-by chapels. I've always dreamed of a big wedding, and he understood, so he nixed the idea of Vegas. Plus, my mother would have killed us both if we eloped.

People were gathered in the church, waiting for the ceremony to begin.

"Lily, where's your sister?"

"I'm not sure, mom. She said she had to go get something and that she'd be right back."

"She's your maid of honor, and she needs to be here; the ceremony's about to start."

I sighed and headed out of the dressing room. I walked down the long hallway that connected to a small kitchen. I figured she probably went out behind the church to have a cigarette, so I proceeded through the kitchen and stopped when I heard a noise coming from one of the rooms off to the side. I put my hand on the knob and slowly turned it as I pushed opened the door. Nothing had prepared me for what I saw.

I pulled the door shut, and I ran out of the church. My heart was racing, and my stomach felt sick. I heard my mother's voice following me from behind. I stopped when she asked me to. I put my hand on my head and paced in circles, not believing what I just saw. My breathing was rapid as I looked up and saw Hunter standing there, looking at me, and my sister standing behind him. Tears began to stream down my face as he slowly started walking towards me. I put my right hand up before he took three steps.

"Don't you dare come near me, you bastard!" I screamed.

"Lily, Hunter, what the hell is going on?" my mother asked.

I stood there, pointing my finger. "Why don't you ask that cheating bastard over there and his dirty whore standing behind him?!" I spat.

My mother turned her head and looked at my sister, Brynn. She stood there, shaking her head; then looked at Hunter. By this time, a crowd of people had emerged from the church and were gathered around to see what all the commotion was. The way my mother was looking at Brynn and Hunter gave me the feeling that she knew what was going on between them.

"Lily, please let me—"Hunter started to say.

"Don't you ever say a fucking word to me again!" I screamed, cutting him off.

I stood there, feeling about as small as an ant, and raised my arms up in the air. "Well, it looks like there isn't going to be a wedding today, folks! Unless, my whore of a sister over there wants to marry this cheating bastard!" I yelled as I pointed to Hunter.

"Lily! That's enough!" my mother commanded.

I looked at her with disgrace and slowly walked towards her. "You knew, didn't you? You knew they were screwing behind my back!"

She stared at me with a look of guilt. She didn't have to say a word; her reaction said it all. I shook my head as I looked at my sister who was standing on the steps, crying. "Why are you crying? Isn't this what you wanted? You can have him, baby sister, because the two of you were made for each other!"

I ripped off my veil and threw it on the ground as I turned on my heels and stomped away. Giselle and Gretchen followed behind, and we took the limo back to their hotel room.

We stepped into the hotel room, and I immediately sat on the edge of the bed. I was still in my wedding dress. The only tears that fell were the ones outside the church. I was still in shock until Giselle sat down next to me and told me that it was ok to cry. I broke down as she held me. Gretchen walked over and sat on the other side as all three of us hugged each other.

"It's going to be ok, Lily," Gretchen whispered.

"How could he do this to me?" I sobbed.

"He's an asshole, and it's better that you found out now," Giselle said.

"She's right, honey, it's better now than five years

from now," Gretchen spoke.

I sniffled as Giselle handed me some tissues. "What are you going to do now?" Gretchen asked.

"Gretchen!" Giselle scolded.

"It's ok. I don't know what I'm going to do. I can't go back home, and I can't face my family. I can't believe my mother knew about Hunter and Brynn. How could she do that to me after what my father did to her?"

"I don't know, sweetie, it's pretty fucked up that she knew, and your sister, my god, why would she do that to you?"

"I feel like I'm going to be sick," I said as I sprang from the bed and into the bathroom, shutting the door behind me.

***

I stayed in the hotel room for an entire week. I didn't get out of bed except to use the bathroom. I kept my phone off and gave strict instructions to Giselle and Gretchen not to let anyone know where I was staying. They went out and bought me a new cell phone so that we could keep in touch, because they needed to get back to California for their jobs. I ordered room service when I felt like it, but I mostly stared at the ceiling, thinking about how much my life sucked. I cried until it felt like my eyes were going to fall out, and I didn't understand why Hunter would do that to me. Oh wait, yes I do. It's because he's a man, and that's what men do. They're cheating, lying bastards who can't commit to one woman. Are all men like that? I'm starting to believe they are. Then, there was my sister.

***

It was Wednesday, so I knew my mother would be at her charity meeting and that my sister would be having lunch with her friends. It was something they did every Wednesday. As the cab pulled up to the house, I stared at it for a minute through the window.

"Miss, are you getting out?" the driver asked.

I looked at him, and it took my brain a minute to register what he asked. "Yeah, I'm sorry." I paid him the cab fare, got out of the cab, and stood in front of the long winding driveway that led to the only house that I've known my entire life. I slowly entered the house, making sure no one was home. I couldn't face my family; not after what they've done to me. I went upstairs to my room, quickly grabbed my suitcases from the closet, and began throwing only the necessities inside. I needed to do this quick before someone came home. I grabbed a handful of clothes from my closet, my makeup, bras, underwear, and shoes. I had two suitcases packed and ready to go. I opened the top drawer of my desk, pulled out my bank book, and I stood in the doorway, looking at my room. I headed down the stairs with my suitcases. As I was approaching the front door, it opened, and my mother walked in. She froze when she saw me, and tears started to fill her eyes.

"Lily, my baby, I was so worried about you. Where have you been?"

I looked at her with a stern look, and I instantly felt sick to my stomach. "It doesn't matter where I've been. The only thing that matters is I'm gone and out of this family forever. What you did to me, by not telling me about Brynn and Hunter, is unforgivable. You helped me plan my wedding, knowing he was fucking my little sister. You were going to let me marry a cheater and a liar. What kind of mother are you?!" I started to cry.

"Lily, please, you have to understand that I was trying to protect you, and he promised me that it was over," she said as she walked towards me with her arms out.

"Don't you dare take another step!" I snapped. "I'm nothing like you, and I won't live my life like you either."

I walked out the front door, stopped, and turned around, staring at my mother as she stood there, crying. "This family is *dead* to me. Tell my little sister that I hope both her and Hunter live happily ever after. Have a nice life, mother." I threw my suitcases in the back of my Explorer, got in, and started the truck as my mother came running out of the house after me.

"Please, Lily, I'm sorry; don't do this to us. You're going to regret it."

"The only thing I regret is ever being a part of this lying, cheating family!" I spat as I peeled out of the driveway and headed as far away from this place as I could. The only thing I knew was that I couldn't stay in Seattle anymore. It was time for me to disappear and start a new life.

I drove for about three hours until my gas light came on. I had reached Portland, Oregon. I pulled into a gas station and opened my purse to get my credit card; then I froze when I saw the two tickets to Aruba, which was supposed to be my honeymoon. We were supposed to leave tomorrow because Hunter couldn't get two weeks off the day after the wedding. I filled up the Explorer with gas and drove down the road to a mini outdoor mall. I took out my camera and decided I was going to take pictures of every place I stopped. I wanted to make a scrapbook of the journey to my new life. I took pictures of the shops, the signs, and the people all around. It was a beautiful, warm sunny day, and I noticed a café with tables that sat outside. I wasn't really hungry, but it had been several hours since I last ate. I took a seat at an open table and then placed my order with the waitress. I was looking around, taking in the fresh air, when I noticed a couple sitting a few tables over from me. They were holding hands, and laughing. The guy was hot; there was no doubt about that, and his girlfriend was very pretty. There was something about his smile that struck me in more places than one. They looked happy, and from what I could see, they were very much in love. I grabbed my camera and snapped a picture of them.

I ate lunch, had a couple glasses of iced tea, and reached for my purse to pay the bill. The tickets fell out and onto the cement floor. I reached down, picked them up, and held them in my hand, staring at them. I left some money on the table and walked over to the happy couple that I'd been watching since I sat down.

"Hi, I know this is weird, but I have two airline tickets to Aruba. The flight leaves tomorrow, and I want you to have them."

They both looked at me like I was crazy.

"You aren't going?" the woman asked in confusion.

"No, actually, something came up, so my fiancé and I aren't able to go. I don't want them to go to waste, and you two look like you would enjoy Aruba together."

She looked at him, and they both looked at me. "Let me pay you for the tickets," the guy said as he reached into his pocket to pull out his wallet.

"No, please, just take them. I don't want your money. Just promise me that you'll have a good time," I said as I put the tickets on the table and started to walk away.

"Wait!" the girl yelled. "Thank you." She smiled.

"Consider it a gift, and just pay it forward someday." I smiled as I walked back to my Explorer.

1

One Year Later…

I inserted the key into the lock and unlocked the door. I slowly turned the handle and lightly pushed the door open as I stepped inside my new apartment. I set my suitcases down and took a deep breath. I flipped the light switch on the wall next to the door and looked around. The furniture that I ordered online had arrived, and it was scattered all over the room. I rented this apartment based off the pictures showcased on the internet. I walked around and inspected the place. The light gray walls and white moldings gave the place a classic look. The eggplant color couch and loveseat I bought matched perfectly, as did the glass coffee table and end tables. I walked down the hall and into my bedroom. I flipped the light switch and stared at the empty space. The bedroom set was being delivered tomorrow. It was late, and I was exhausted as I drove fourteen hours straight from Portland to Santa Monica. My Explorer was filled with boxes, but they would have to wait until the morning. At that moment, I just wanted to feel the comfort of my new couch.

I spent the last year in Portland when my car broke down, and it took two weeks to get it repaired. I guess you could say the place grew on me, and I really didn't have any other place to go. I rented an apartment, took a job as a freelance photographer for the local newspaper, and I was a substitute teacher for a few months at one of the local elementary schools. How did I end up in Santa Monica? The local newspaper shut down, and my gig as a substitute teacher had ended when the regular teacher came back from maternity leave. Giselle called me one day and said that her aunt Chris, the principal of an elementary school in Santa Monica, was looking for a long-term substitute teacher and that I should call her. So, I did, and that's how I ended up here.

Giselle and Gretchen live in Santa Monica, and I was excited to be living near them again. They're twins, and we've been best friends for as long as I could remember. I met them when I was six years old, when they moved into the house next door. Their father was an investment banker, and their mother was a model in her younger days. Giselle and Gretchen followed in their mother's footsteps. With their 5'10" height and size 6 bodies, they were made to be models. I was envious of their deep brown eyes and their long, straight brown hair. Our mothers used to call us the three musketeers because we were inseparable. We did everything together, and we were always there when the other one needed us. The twins were my rock, and no matter what exotic place their job took them to, we talked every day.

***

I opened my eyes and was startled by the music I heard, coming through the wall. I grabbed my phone and looked at the time; it was 3:00 a.m. I had been sleeping for about two hours, which had become the norm for me since I caught Hunter and Brynn together in the church. My mind's on permanent rewind, and every time I closed my eyes, that scene played over and over again. I got up from the couch, grabbed my purse, and walked to the bathroom. I wanted to wash my face, but I forgot that all my towels and washcloths were packed away in one of the boxes that sat in the Explorer. I took the brush out of my purse and ran it through my long, blonde hair. I searched for a rubber band and pulled my hair into a high ponytail. As I looked at myself in the mirror, I couldn't help but notice the bags underneath my blue-gray eyes. I really needed a shower, so I put on my shoes, grabbed my keys, and headed towards the Explorer. As I stepped out into the hallway of my apartment, I stood there and stared at the door from which the blaring music was coming from. I shook my head, rolled my eyes, and headed to my SUV for the box that was labeled: *BATHROOM.*

I lifted the box out of the Explorer, and then carried it to the door of the apartment building. I set the box down for a minute while I opened the door with my key. As I was inserting the key, the door opened, and I stumbled back, nearly being knocked down.

"I'm sorry, miss, I didn't see you there," he apologized.

He looked at me and then at the box on the ground. "Are you moving in?" he asked as he looked at his watch.

"Yes, I just got here a few hours ago, and I haven't had a chance to get the boxes from my truck," I answered.

"It's nice to meet you; I'm Sam," he said as he held out his hand.

"Hi, I'm Lily. It's nice to meet you too."

"Let me grab that box for you," he offered as he bent down to pick it up.

"No, that's alright, I've got it," I said as I put my hand in front of him.

"Don't be ridiculous. Let me carry the box for you since I almost knocked you on your ass with the door." He smiled.

It was the middle of the night, and I was arguing with a hot guy over a box. "Fine; my apartment's right there,"

I said as I pointed to my door.

Sam looked at me and smiled. "Well, look at that; looks like we're neighbors."

I opened the door for him as he stepped inside my apartment and set the box down on the floor. "So, you're the one playing the loud music at 3:00 a.m.?" I asked.

"Sorry about that," he said as shrugged his shoulders. "I'll tell Lucky to keep it down."

"I'd appreciate that. Thanks for the help with the box," I said as I shut the door.

I spent the next hour unpacking the box and putting away the towels. I organized all my bathroom items and then took a hot, relaxing bubble bath. My hands began to wander as it had been a while since my battery operated boyfriend and I had a date. As soon as I was finished, I got out of the tub, wrapped a towel around me, and walked into the living room where my suitcases were. I opened one suitcase and pulled out a pair of jean shorts and a navy blue tank top. I grabbed my phone from the couch and looked at the time; it was 6:00 a.m. Giselle and Gretchen were coming over to help me unpack around 8:00 a.m., and the bedroom set was being delivered between 9:00 a.m. and 11:00 a.m. I blow-dried my hair then put it back up in a high ponytail. I put on some light makeup and then decided to go for some coffee.

I stepped out of my apartment at the same time Sam did his. We both looked at each other, and he smiled. "Don't you ever sleep?" he asked.

"I should be asking you the same thing." I smiled back.

Sam was hot; there was no question about it. He stood around six feet tall with a great muscular body, sandy brown hair, and brown eyes. He definitely fit the Santa Monica image.

"Where are you off to so early in the morning?" he asked.

It really wasn't any of his business, but he was being nice, so I felt the neighborly thing to do was to be nice in return.

"I'm off to find some much needed caffeine," I replied as I stepped out of the building door, and he followed behind me.

"Me too," he said. "I went to make some coffee, but the bag was empty. I hate it when Luke doesn't tell me we're out of coffee."

"Luke?" I asked.

"Yeah, he's my BF and roommate. Hey, would you like to go get some coffee together?" he asked with a smile.

I studied him. Sam seemed like a really nice guy, and he was gay, so I didn't have to worry about him hitting on me.

"Sure, I'll go with you, but we have to make it quick; my girlfriends are coming over to help mc unpack."

I hopped into his truck, and we drove down the road to a coffee house called 'Brewsters.' We walked inside, and Sam was instantly greeted by the girl behind the counter.

"Morning, Sam! Who's your friend?" she asked as she was wiping down the counter.

"Morning, Jamie! This is Lily; she just moved in next door. Lily, this is my cousin, Jamie; she owns this lovely coffee house."

Jamie wiped her hand dry and held it out to me as I gently shook it.

"It's nice to meet you, Lily. Are you new in town?"

"Yes, I just moved here from Portland last night," I replied.

"Great, well welcome to Santa Monica and to Brewsters! What can I get you?" she asked.

"I'll just have a large black coffee." I smiled. I looked over at Sam and found him staring at me. "What?" I asked.

"That's how Luke drinks his coffee. I don't

understand how you can drink it with no sugar or cream. We argue about it all the time."

"Everyone has different coffee taste, Sam," Jamie said.

"Let me pay for your coffee," I said to Sam.

"It's on the house." Jamie smiled as she handed us our coffees. "Cheap-ass, Sam, over here never pays. Consider it a 'welcome to Santa Monica gift.'"

"Thanks, Jamie!" Sam smiled as he grabbed a bag of coffee from the shelf. "I'm taking a bag home; I owe you!"

Jamie rolled her eyes. "He owes me every week." She laughed.

"Thank you, Jamie. It was nice to meet you." I smiled as I held up my coffee cup.

"It was to meet you too!"

I walked out of Brewsters and climbed into the truck. "Your cousin is really nice," I said.

"Yeah, she's more like my sister. She came to live with me and my family when she was eight years old. Her mom and dad were drug dealers who got caught, and they were sent to prison."

"Are they still in prison?" I asked.

"Yeah, 20 years later, and they're still there. She hasn't seen them in all these years either."

We arrived back at the apartment building, and I got out of the truck. I walked over to my Explorer and set my coffee cup on the hood. I took the keys from my purse and unlocked it. Sam followed me.

"Let me give you a hand with those boxes," he offered.

"That's alright, Sam. Go enjoy your coffee. I can handle this."

He walked over to the back of the Explorer. "Nah, come on, Lily; just let me help. It's the neighborly thing to do anyway."

I sighed and unwillingly opened the hatch. Sam smiled, grabbed a box, and headed towards the apartment building. I stepped ahead of him so that I could hold open the door. Before I got up to the door, it swung open, and a guy stood there, staring at me.

"Luke, you're just in time; hold this box," Sam said as he handed it to him.

"What are you doing?" Luke asked. "I woke up, and you were gone. By the way, there's no coffee left."

"Yeah, I know; I just picked some up at Brewsters. I have the bag in my truck. By the way, this is Lily; she's our new next-door neighbor."

Luke looked at me. "Hey," he said as he quickly looked away.

"Hey," I replied back.

I couldn't help but stare at him. He stood in the doorway—all six feet of him—in ripped jeans and a gray muscle shirt. He was barefoot, and his short, brown hair was messy. He was definitely one of the hottest men that I'd ever seen. You could tell he worked out by the muscle and definition in his arms and shoulders. He had a Celtic cross tattooed on his left bicep, with wings behind it. Thank *God* he was gay. I felt rather uncomfortable because Luke didn't seem as friendly as Sam did.

"Lily, go unlock your apartment door so that we can get these boxes in there," Sam said.

I walked past Luke and caught him staring at me. The minute I looked at him, he turned away. As I unlocked the door and opened it, I stepped outside and held the building door open so that Luke could set the box down in my apartment. He did just that and then went inside his apartment and shut the door behind him without saying a word.

"What's his problem?" I asked Sam.

"Just ignore him. He's not much of a morning person, that's all."

I couldn't shake the feeling that he seemed familiar to me, but I knew it wasn't possible. Just as Sam and I were bringing in the last of the boxes, Giselle and Gretchen pulled up. I haven't seen them in over three months, so I put down my box and ran over to them as they got out of the car. I hugged Gretchen first and then Giselle.

"I'm so happy you moved to Santa Monica," Giselle said as she hugged me tight.

"Me too," I said as my eyes began to swell with tears.

"Who's the hot guy that's walking towards us?" Gretchen smiled as she pushed her hair back behind her ear.

"Hello, ladies." Sam smiled.

"Sam, this is Giselle, and this is Gretchen; they're my two best friends."

"It's a pleasure to meet the both of you," Sam said as he held out his hand to each of them.

"Sam lives next door, and he's been helping me bring the boxes in," I said.

"We also went out for coffee this morning," he blurted out.

Giselle looked at me and smiled. "Did you hear that, Gretchen? Lily went out for coffee with a guy."

"I sure did, sis!" Gretchen smiled at me.

I turned and looked at Sam. "Don't listen to them. Thank you for your help; I appreciate it."

"No problem. If you need anything, just knock on my

door or wall." He smiled.

I grabbed Gretchen and Giselle's hands and led them into my new apartment.

Made in the USA
Charleston, SC
14 July 2015